PLAYING THE GAME

EILEEN DREYER

OLIVER-HEBER BOOKS

Published by Oliver-Heber Books

0 9 8 7 6 5 4 3 2 1

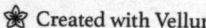 Created with Vellum

PRAISE FOR EILEEN DREYER

"Can You Get Me Out Of Here Before They Get Me?"

From nowhere, a man had leaped into the passenger seat of Kelly's little convertible. He was probably the most handsome man she'd ever seen. She suddenly realized she recognized him from someplace but even so, her reaction was instinctive.

"That line hasn't worked in years. Get out of my car!"

"I'm serious," he insisted. "Look."

She did, and she saw what he meant. Barely a block away, a pack of people armed with cameras and microphones was bearing down on them. Kelly slammed her MG into gear and took off.

"Thanks," he said with relief. "They almost got us."

"Are you running from the police?"

He chuckled. "I was waiting for them. They got there just a little too late to help."

"Then what was that crowd for?"

Her question was met by an odd silence. "You don't know who I am, do you?"

AUTHOR'S NOTE

Playing the Game was my first book published in 1986. I had the option of bringing it forward in time, but I find I like it just where it is. You can think of it as a historical if you want. A time when we weren't all connected by cellphones and internet. I hope you enjoy a place not so long ago, but still so very different.

CHAPTER 1

Kelly Byrne saw the beauty of the approaching night and ached with sudden loneliness. By the time she pulled her MG into traffic, the sun had disappeared behind the cityscape, but the light had not yet faded from the sky. Office windows up and down the street reflected the golds and carmines of the autumn sunset. The evening star winked to life just below where a crescent moon rode a sea of piercing blue. With the soft earthy aroma of the air, Kelly could almost imagine that it was spring, not fall, that the pleasures of summer could still be anticipated, and that she would still find Michael when she opened the door.

But it wasn't spring. And Michael wouldn't be there anymore.

Kelly sat at a stoplight, no longer seeing the sky, waiting for a light she wasn't really aware of. She took a long calming breath, not noticing that the people in cars around her had begun to turn toward the first sounds of a disturbance.

In the back of her mind, she supposed she heard the growing clamor, the shouting. She just didn't pay any attention because her mind was preoccupied with thoughts of Michael. She'd been alone for almost two years. She shouldn't still be reacting this way.

Suddenly, the car lurched. Kelly whipped around, catapulted back to the present. She heard the noise now, a milling, babbling sound that rose from behind her. It sounded like the dissonance of an excited mob. But the noise wasn't what held her astonished attention. What had suddenly appeared next to her did. Or to be more precise, who.

From nowhere, a man had literally leaped into the passenger seat of her little convertible. Kelly turned to see him pulling the paraphernalia she'd collected on her day off out of his way. He heaped four boxes of tea, two stuffed animals and a quilted wall hanging onto his lap. Holding a stuffed animal in one hand, he reached under himself with the other and pulled out a hat that said "I JUST ESCAPED FROM THE ST LOUIS ZOO." Kelly opened her mouth to scream.

He reacted quickly, hands outstretched, a koala pointing back toward the noise. "Can you get me out of here...anywhere, before they get me?"

He was probably the most handsome man Kelly had ever seen. In the brief time it took for him to speak, she took in soft, curly dark hair cut close to the head, blue-green eyes and a face that had been built to be craggy, but softened easily with his flashing smile. She knew just as suddenly that she knew him from somewhere. She just couldn't remember where. Even so, her reaction was instinctive.

"That line hasn't worked since Harrison Ford tried it in *The Fugitive*. Get out of my car."

"I'm serious," he insisted. The honeyed tones of his baritone voice strained for credibility. "Look."

He gestured again with the koala.

With a pained expression for his benefit, she did. And she saw what he meant. Barely a block away, a pack of people with cameras and microphones was bearing down on her little MG. The stoplight changed, and the car behind her reminded her of it. She turned back to the man next to her for explanation.

"The light changed," he prompted easily, an eye still to the oncoming crowd.

The car behind her repeated the message more emphatically. With no small amount of irritation, Kelly slammed the car into gear and took off. Her companion took one more look at his pursuers and settled back into the seat, Kelly's zoo hat perched precariously on his head.

"Turn right," he suggested.

Not knowing exactly why, she did. He smiled at her, his teeth even and white. A news anchor, she thought. Maybe a new one. She watched so little television, it was hard to tell. He was dressed like an off-duty county lawyer, early preppy-casual with an open-necked Oxford shirt and pullover sweater that complemented tight, pre-faded jeans.

"Thanks," he intoned. "They almost got your license number."

Kelly shot him a look, suddenly frightened. "Are you running from the police?"

His eyes opened with almost comic incredulity as he chuckled. It was a pleasant, musical sound. "I was waiting for them. They got there a little too late to help."

"Then what was that crowd for? Did you insult their religious leader? Steal their lottery tickets?"

This time, her question was met by an odd silence. It forced her to look over at him. She was caught again by the nagging feeling of familiarity. She also became aware of his size. He towered over her, his knees drawn ridiculously close to his chest to enable him to fit into the seat. His shoulders were broad and strong, his arms powerful.

Something about him made her uncomfortable, unsettled. It was as if he had an aura, an electrical field that surrounded him, and she had stumbled too near it. It made the hairs on the back of her neck bristle. If she had been the type to blush, she knew she would have.

"You don't know who I am, do you?" he asked with an odd smile.

If only he hadn't said that. Nothing stiffened Kelly's spine faster than the self-importance of words like that. The hospital in whose emergency room she worked was situated in the more affluent suburbs of St. Louis, and lines like "Do you know who I am?" were used with irritating regularity. When her unexpected companion had the poor judgment to wield the challenge on her, she pulled abruptly to the curb and turned to him with ice in her eyes.

"I don't *care* who you are."

Whatever she had expected his reaction to be, and in most people it usually ranged from irritation to outrage, she was in for a surprise. He was absolutely delighted.

"Wonderful!" he said laughing, his eyes alight with mischief.

She still wasn't impressed. And she wasn't about to ask the question that nagged ever more insistently at her. Every time he moved or spoke, even with that dumb little hat perched so absurdly on his head, he struck a feeling of déjà vu in her. Damn it, she knew him. She just couldn't for the life of her remember from where.

No matter. She wasn't about to wait long enough to find out.

"All right," she said evenly, motioning to the usual bustle of the evening sidewalk beyond him. "The hounds have lost the scent. You can go home, now."

He turned to follow the direction of her gesture, and then looked back at her with an apologetic grin. "Not really. That's where they found me. I, uh,...I'd rather not go back there for a while."

She considered his smile for a moment. "You'd rather hang around me."

He immediately brightened.

Kelly shook her head. "I don't adopt stray puppies."

"I'll take you to dinner."

"Too late."

He paused to consider. "All right. My name's Matthew...Matthews. Paul Matthews."

The name didn't do a thing to spark recognition. "Why should I know you?"

"Do you watch the news?"

"I work evenings. And thanks, I deal with enough disgusting human behavior without going out of my way to see more."

She tried to sound disparaging, but his smile was infectious. She could feel it tugging at the corners of her own mouth.

He nodded, never taking those softly shaded sea-blue eyes from her. They were dangerously sapping her resistance.

"I, uh...made the news recently," he said. "Business. All the local press covered it. When I got into...back into town tonight, they were all waiting for me. I just flew into the country, and I didn't feel like facing them yet." His rueful grin broadened, gleaming oddly in the deepening dusk and street light. "So, here I am."

The night was closing in, and Kelly was still dressed for an afternoon stroll through the zoo. She wanted to get home before she froze. "Check into a hotel."

He smiled again. "That's what I was trying to do. I saw them at the house and tried to sneak out to a hotel. Somebody squealed."

"Stay with your family."

Another rueful shake of the head.

"Of course." She tilted her head, eyeing him carefully. It was getting very dark now, and he was thrown into colorless shadows, but she could still feel the almost electric sensation of his proximity. She couldn't remember ever reacting to a man like this before, even Michael. Even beautiful, gentle Michael. Yet this man's eyes discarded the importance of the magnetism he must have known he possessed. It frightened and fascinated her. "I suppose you want me to think of something."

"No such thing," he assured her blithely. "I already have a wonderful idea. If you don't have any house rules against visitors, maybe you could put me up for the night. I promise that after that flight today, all I could manage right now is sleep. My body still thinks it's four in the morning. What do you say?"

For a moment, Kelly just stared at him. Then, even as her stomach did a somersault and a little voice deep inside told her she was nuts, she flashed Mr. Matthews a grin and put her car into gear. "Take off my hat. If you lose it, you're going to have to walk back and get it."

It was his turn to show some surprise. "I had you figured for at least a fifteen-minute argument."

Kelly's smile was smug. "Why? You're not going to bother me any. My next-door neighbor's the chief of police. Besides, I'm working tonight."

"Really? What are you, a waitress?"

She shook her head, her eyes on the road. "Madame at a house of ill repute. This is our busiest time of the day."

She was rewarded by another deep chuckle as he doffed her hat and turned to face front. For a moment they rode along the tree-lined streets in silence. The traffic was lighter now, so the driving took less concentration. Kelly could have put the car on automatic pilot. She just wished she'd taken the time to put up the top. She was beginning to shiver with the cold night air. But then if she'd had the top up, the enigmatic Mr. Matthews wouldn't be sharing his electrical field with her.

She had absolutely no idea what she'd gotten herself into. Paul Matthews could very well be a second-story man with a smooth line. Or he could be worse. But then, she'd seen worse. She'd seen all kinds of worse in the years she'd been a nurse, and her common sense told her he wasn't one. And her gut reaction had never been wrong.

"By the way," he suddenly said, "we haven't been properly introduced. I could call you madame, I guess."

"No, that's all right," Kelly demurred. "I think Kelly would be more discreet. Kelly Byrne."

"Kelly," he crooned, his voice absolutely hypnotic. "It's been my pleasure to meet you. I can't thank you enough for taking me in like this."

Before Kelly knew it, he'd reached over to take her

hand. A simple gesture of sincerity. An affirmation. She almost lost control of the car.

It was as if she'd been shocked. He barely touched her. She saw his strong fingers reach over her tiny ones and engulf them gently. She heard his words of sincere thanks. And she lost her breath at the headiness of his touch.

Kelly turned from him, losing his eyes in the night and wondering if she'd been nuts or whether he'd felt it, too. Maybe I've been alone too long, she thought. Maybe I should drop this guy off at the nearest motel and get the hell away from him.

"Where do you live, Kelly?" he asked, facing the road and watching the shadows, the wind picking at his clothes. He'd taken his hand back, and with it the sense of fire. Kelly decided that she'd just been up too long. She hadn't worked enough nights to get used to them, and she'd wasted her sleep time today buying balloons and stuffed koala bears.

Her attention returned to the road. "Here in Webster Groves," she told him. "Off Elm."

"Webster?" He turned abruptly, his posture sharpening. "Isn't that—" Looking about him into the darkness. He stopped just as abruptly. "Wonderful. It's a beautiful place."

What was going on here? He'd just caught himself short, as if afraid to reveal something. Kelly watched him a moment, wondering at his suddenly bland smile. Then she looked back out around her. They were passing Webster College and the Repertory Theatre. The theater was having a special Tennessee Williams tribute that had been sold out for months. Kelly knew; she'd desperately tried to get tickets.

"Yes," she answered slowly, taking another look at him. "Webster's nice. Real Americana. I always thought they filmed those lemonade commercials down the street from me."

"You have a house?"

She nodded. "Not as big as some of the others, but it has a porch on three sides and a real picket fence. And we planted a yardful of azaleas and dogwood."

His question was phrased politely after a brief hesitation. "We?"

Kelly took a minute to answer. She'd turned onto Elm and could see, now, the heavy shadows of the ancient trees for which the street had been named. Carefully manicured lawns stretched away to huge turn-of-the-century Victorian houses where light spilled from scores of windows. Kelly had lived in Webster Groves all her life, and truly coveted the lavish old homes and huge, lush lawns where one could imagine summer parties in bygone days when women wore organdy and crinolines, and horse-drawn carriages carried visitors back and forth on lazy warm afternoons. In the spring the world bound by these quiet streets, would explode with hot color and rich fragrance from the thousands of fruit trees, dogwoods, azaleas and rhododendron that crowded the lawns. Every imaginable bulb would line brick sidewalks, and the air would throb with the sound of insects.

Michael had found their house only four years ago and had led her in blindfolded. To this day, when she thought of that moment, she remembered the echoing emptiness of parquet floors and twelve-foot ceilings, endless windows and a sense of stillness. They'd slept on the floor that first night and made love before the fireplace.

"My husband Michael and I," she said quietly.

"Oh, I didn't know," he said a bit uncomfortably.

"Won't he wonder about me, or did you lie about picking up stray puppies?"

Kelly almost smiled. She'd lied all right. Michael had been a stray puppy. She'd brought him in out of a St. Louis thunderstorm and taken him to her own emergency room when he'd caught pneumonia. So very long ago.

"You don't have to worry. I live alone now."

"Divorced?"

Kelly flared briefly, turning on him, but the question had been an innocent one. After all, that would be the logical assumption these days.

With an effort she let her hackles go down. "No. Widowed. Michael died two years ago."

It had been a call on the red phone. Standard stuff for a Friday night in West County. The paramedics had a trauma from a one-car accident, probably DOA. Nothing special. She hadn't even recognized him until she saw the wedding band she'd bought him in Ireland. They said that she hadn't stop screaming until they held her down and shot her up with IV Valium.

Paul's answering silence was even more uncomfortable. "I'm sorry."

Kelly shrugged, trying to displace memories that hadn't crowded this close in a long time. "It's all right. Well, here we are, the old Byrne homestead."

She turned into her driveway, the headlights sweeping over familiar trees and the chief's ivy-lined sidewalk next door. Paul tumbled from the car and walked around to help her out, his arms full of her packages. Kelly knew that he was big, but she'd had no idea just how big. She could stretch to five feet when she wanted, and Michael at five-foot-eleven had seemed a protective height. This man with the goalpost shoulders absolutely dwarfed her. With those wide shoulders, slim hips and flat belly, he looked like a well-toned athlete. He was grinning down at her as she pulled herself to her full height, which put her eyes right at the third button of his shirt.

"No wonder you drive this little car," he teased. "Where'd you get it, F.A.O. Schwartz?"

"Don't insult the short, pal," she retorted easily as she led him up to the porch. His shoes clattered hollowly on the wooden steps. "It was a short person who invented revenge."

Kelly led him into the house and reached for the light switch. At the front window, an old art deco lamp flooded the room in soft yellow light revealing the simple lines of Kelly's taste. She'd decorated the living room in teal blues and cream to offset the colors of the oriental rug that covered much of the hardwood floor. Blue wing-back chairs flanked the tall graceful fireplace. The divan, in a soft floral pattern, was set against the wall across from the fireplace. Kelly had added two Queen Anne chairs she'd found at a farm auction, and Michael had crafted a delicate sofa-back table for odd books and a vase of flowers. In the large shuttered bay window, the floor lamp kept company with hanging plants.

Kelly caught her reflection in the large beveled mirror that hung over the fireplace. Next to Mr. Matthews, she looked like a munchkin. Even with the *Kaptain Kangaroo* pockets of her uniform full to bursting when she weighed herself at work, she barely topped a hundred-ten pounds. Mr. Matthews easily had a hundred pounds on her. She didn't need the mirror to tell her that her features matched the rest of her look: heart-shaped face, Little Orphan Annie eyes, freckles over fair skin and her small upturned nose. In my next life, she thought with a scowl, I'm going to be blond. And at least five-eight.

"No wonder you like the house so well," Paul murmured, bringing her back with a snap. "This is a beautiful place."

When she turned to answer, she was plagued again by that feeling of familiarity. It was as if she were trying to remember a dream from the night before and could only pull back feelings instead of pictures. "Thank you."

Her voice sounded stiff. He didn't seem to notice. For a few minutes he wandered around, peeking out of the dining room windows and running his hand along the soft oak of the banister that led up from the entrance hallway to the floor above.

"You want the whole tour?"

Paul smiled his acceptance, and Kelly led him through the house: upstairs to the three bedrooms, the master suite with the canopied four-poster, and the bathroom with the original freestanding bathtub. Downstairs to the family room where photos Kelly and Michael had taken cluttered the walls, and the red-and-white country kitchen, where Kelly offered to brew some coffee. She caught her guest rubbing at his eyes.

"If you're serious about getting that sleep," she suggested, "you should forget coffee and head straight for the guest room."

He nodded. "I think I will." When he stood to make his way upstairs, he paused. "I owe you a big favor, Kelly. Thanks."

She brushed aside his words. "Give me some useful stock tips sometime."

He looked up, his face caught between amusement

and caution, and Kelly knew for certain that his story had been fabrication.

Half an hour later after apprising her startled neighbor on her surprise guest—Kelly wasn't completely idiotic--she sat alone in the kitchen trying to drink enough coffee to keep her awake till dawn and pondering the madness that had urged her into taking a strange man into her house for...how long? She caught herself looking up toward the room where he now slept. They hadn't really come to any conclusions about that, had they? In fact, the elusive Mr. Matthews hadn't been conclusive about much at all.

The funny thing was, Kelly didn't feel in the least bothered by it. This stranger had blown an odd kind of fresh air into her life. After Michael's death, she'd pulled tightly into a shell just to survive. Nightmares of that night still followed her too closely. Only recently had she started going out at all, mostly at the insistence of her friend Missy. And then only with Rich Weber, a resident at work.

She and Rich had started going out to fill dead space on Saturday nights, and the relationship hadn-ever progressed any further. Rich was quiet, dependable and comfortably free of surprises. They had remained good friends, with no demands or expectations. Kelly had certainly never reacted to his touch or presence the way she had to Paul's.

Again she caught herself looking up as if able to divine some kind of answer to the uncomfortably exhilarating puzzle who'd walked into her life. Paul. Paul Matthews. She had the distinct feeling that even his name was only close to the truth. Well, she thought pragmatically as she downed the rest of her coffee and stood to get ready for work, the way things go tonight,

I probably won't have much chance to worry about it, and by morning he'll probably be gone.

~

SHE WAS RIGHT ABOUT WORK, anyway. It had been a beautiful day, and true to form, everyone in and around the city had done his level best to cram too much into maybe one last weekend. And every one of them seemed to end up in the ER. Kelly walked into a full-blown disaster and didn't so much as sit down for close to seven hours. By then, her eyes burned from her cavalier lack of sleep, and she rubbed them as she gulped at even more coffee. A pile of unfinished charts awaited her attention next to the pile Missy was working on. Beverly Post, the night secretary, had waded into the weekend papers and was doing a dramatic reading of some of the more interesting stories to help keep them all awake.

Kelly almost wished she hadn't sat down at all. The adrenaline that had pushed her so far was dying hard in her tired veins, and the longer she sat, the more she just wanted to lay her head down and sleep. Even Beverly's entertainment and Missy's correspondingly dry wit did little to keep her alert.

"Holy crap!" Beverly gasped.

Missy turned. Kelly tried her best to keep the printed words before her in focus. "God, Missy," Beverly called, waving the paper at her. "Look at this, you're just not going to believe it!"

Missy obliged, moving to look over the secretary's shoulder. A moment later she added her own surprised noises.

"Oh, come on, honey, that's not possible," she objected. "I never would have recognized him. And I'm the one who swore that nobody could mistake Superman just because he put on glasses."

"If that's what he looks like now, I can't wait to see the movie. It's supposed to be out next week some time."

"Honey, I'd pay money to see Matt Hennessy read the yellow pages for two hours."

Kelly had heard the conversation in passing, but hadn't had the energy to pay attention to it. Then Missy dragged her into the act.

"Kelly, I know you've seen Matt Hennessy's movies."

She nodded absently. "That's probably because you dragged me to see *The Outer Edge* four times."

"Well then, take a look at this."

With a creaking groan, Kelly got to her feet and took the necessary three steps to Beverly's other shoulder. Missy pointed a red nail down at the twin pictures that covered the top third of the Sunday magazine section.

"He shaved his beard and cut his hair for his new picture. And I thought I'd miss all that hair. Seems like a waste of good face now."

Kelly got one good look before her knees gave out and she landed precariously on the edge of her chair. Neither Missy nor Beverly noticed; their eyes were riveted by the handsome face that smiled from the pictures. But Kelly felt her stomach plummet and then lurch with sick surprise.

She'd just recognized the man she'd invited to sleep in her house.

CHAPTER 2

K elly drove home in dumbfounded silence. She couldn't seem to get past the fact that Matt Hennessy was the man who was asleep in her guest room. Things like that just didn't happen, at least not to people like Kelly.

Matt Hennessy—Paul Matthew Hennessy to be precise—had burst onto the scene a scant four years ago in an action-adventure picture that had been thoroughly panned by the critics and overwhelmingly attended by the public. His performance as the post-civilization loner who struggled to survive against great odds had won him a place among maternal instincts and masculine pride everywhere. Kelly had seen the picture with Michael and had promptly fallen under the Hennessy spell along with everyone else. She'd found his touch of vulnerability just as appealing as his good looks.

Now, four movies later, Matt Hennessy had a firm hold on not only legendary fame, but the grudging respect and admiration of the critics who had earlier derided him. He was the hottest thing since bicycles. And he was asleep in Kelly's bedroom.

She still couldn't believe that she hadn't given it away at work. Bev and Missy had been too preoccupied by the pictures to pay attention to her abrupt silence, so that she'd had time enough to regain her equilibrium before facing them. By then she'd decided to keep the information to herself, at least until she got the chance to face Mr. Hennessy alone with it. She wanted to get his explanation before they got hers.

To be truthful, she wasn't at all that sure just how she was going to react to seeing Matt Hennessy. She'd talked to him last night, but that had been different. Then he had been Paul Matthews—handsome, magnetic and a trifle mysterious. But not famous. Not *that* famous. The magnitude of her situation stuck in the cogs of her brain like a misplaced wrench and turned it into soup.

Matt Hennessy.

Her stomach lurched.

When Kelly opened the front door, he was the first thing she saw. Paul. Matt. Matt Hennessy. He stood by the stairs as if he'd been waiting for her, his eyes bright and alert, his clothing amazingly neat and tidy. Only a faint stubble of beard betrayed the fact that he'd really been there all night.

Seeing him, Kelly couldn't believe that she hadn't recognized him right away. After all the times she'd seen his movies, she'd thought she had memorized those eyes. They turned on her now with a delight that threatened to take the strength out of her knees.

The indignation in her voice surprised her. "Why didn't you tell me you were...?" She never got the words out. Matt suddenly had his arms out to her, rushing to her as if he'd waited for her all his life.

"Kelly!"

Before she had a chance to react, he swept her into his arms, his mouth crushing down on hers. She moved to protest, to pull away. What the hell did he think he was doing? This wasn't a scene out of a bad movie. She brought her hands up against him, fully intending to slap him upside his head and then make him go back where he came from. It infuriated her that she might have misjudged him so badly.

But she couldn't slap him. Within the immeasurably brief time it takes dry kindling to spark into flame, his touch ignited her. Kelly could do no more than stand before it, the shock numbing her mind. Matt pulled her to him, his powerful arms all but squeezing the breath from her. The touch of him, the smell of him, the rock hardness of his chest against her hands stilled her. His lips, so soft for their power, silenced her. He cupped her head in one hand, and she could feel the charge of his fingers against her scalp. Instinctively she closed her eyes.

Matt held her for what seemed like an eternity before he moved his mouth to her ear. "You have company."

Kelly hardly took notice. The tickling of his lips at her ear, the heat of his breath against the nape of her very sensitive neck, sent fresh shock waves through her. She was sure that he could hear her heart. It raced along like a trip-hammer, and she was in imminent danger of hyperventilating.

Matt straightened and turned, his arm still possessively held tight around her waist. Kelly was thankful for that at least. At the moment, she wouldn't have trusted her legs to keep her up. She saw Matt smile beyond her and moved to follow the direction of his gaze when she suffered her second or third major surprise of the still-early morning.

Rich. Oh, damn. Looking as if he'd just committed some indiscretion, the young resident stood stiffly on the oriental rug, his bike leaning against the front wall. He didn't live far away, and it wasn't all that unusual for him to cycle over unannounced for a visit. He would never have thought to call ahead to check Kelly's plans. She never had any. She could see the acute embarrassment in his gentle brown eyes, and it brought a rare flush to her cheeks.

As angry as she was frightened by her reaction to Matt, she fought desperately to right her senses. It wasn't fair that he should do this. Had he hurt Rich intentionally, or just thought it a cute prank? Whatever his reasons, she could well see the results. Her good opinion of Matt Hennessy seemed more in jeopardy by the minute.

When she tried to find voice for explanation, she could only see how pale Rich was—with his average, almost blond good looks and quiet sincere personality —when compared to Matt.

The unbidden thought brought a lurch of terror she couldn't comprehend.

Matt didn't waste any time on explanations. He turned back to Kelly, his eyes solicitous and happy. "I'm sorry I didn't call." Sincerity dripped from every word. "I really didn't get the chance. Suddenly I found myself with a free week and an available plane. Thought I'd surprise you."

So that was it. He was inventing another Paul Matthews. Was this the same one as last night, or did he fancy someone new?

"You surprised me, all right," she managed, her voice a little breathless.

That made her even more angry. Rich was her friend, and Matt was patronizing them both with his stupid little game. She had to let Rich know that. She had to let Rich know that the hurt in his eyes was unwarranted.

She tried to get away from Matt, but he held her tight.

"Rich—"

Matt interrupted easily. "Oh, we introduced ourselves already. I was just telling Rich how you and I met, Kelly."

Oh, she thought with no little sarcasm, just how was that? She settled for a deadpan delivery of, "It seems like only yesterday."

"Kelly, do you realize that it's been almost six weeks since I've seen you? You look more beautiful than ever." He turned a dazzling smile on the bemused Rich. "I know four sheikhs who would sell their souls for someone with eyes as blue as Kelly's. I fell for her the minute I saw her." He turned back to Kelly. "You know, you never wrote me that Rich was a doctor. He's been telling me all about it, and I had to tell him how envious I was. Did I ever tell you that I wanted to be a doctor?"

"Gee no, you didn't."

She got away from him this time and gave herself some breathing room. The morning seemed ten degrees cooler beyond his reach. Kelly took a slow, deep breath to calm her still-tingling nerves, and turned purposefully to Rich. She saw in his eyes the same reaction she'd had on meeting Matt, where do I know this guy? She wondered just what he'd do if she told him, if she just said, "Rich, he's giving you a line. He's Matt Hennessy..."

She was really about to say it, would have, if Matt hadn't turned to her just then. Even as he talked on about his life and Rich's work, he begged his cause to her. For the briefest of moments the glibness died in his eyes, and Kelly saw the plea revealed beneath. Its sincerity stopped her.

Matt rambled on about his imaginary import-export business and Kelly watched in silence. She supposed that she could explain it to Rich after Matt had gone. It wasn't really that much of a sin for a world-famous person to want to escape his notoriety for just a little while.

"I never got the grades," Matt was saying to Rich, "I ended up in business school. USC."

That much was fact. Kelly had read it in an interview somewhere. Matt certainly seemed to know how to appropriately craft the truth.

"Listen, Rich," she said. "Why don't you stay for coffee?"

"Oh no, I..." Rich made a move to leave, the discomfort of the situation resurfacing on his pleasant features. "I'd just stopped by to see if...uh, you'd wanted to go riding, Kelly. I forgot you worked last night. I'll, uh, just..."

"Nonsense," Matt retorted with an expansive sweep of the arm. "You shouldn't come all this way without sampling Kelly's delicious coffee."

Rich's deadpan reaction was enough to bring a grin back to Kelly's eyes. She walked over and took him by the arm, turning him back away from the front door. As she passed Matt on her way to the kitchen, she stopped.

"You could use my coffee to pave roads, and Rich knows it. And," she added, a finger to Matt's chest for emphasis, the little game giving her unwanted exhilaration, "so do you."

Matt's silent thanks was eloquent.

The conversation in the kitchen turned out to be

surprisingly congenial. Matt had such a good time fabricating his life with breezy half-truths and elaborations that it was difficult not to be swept along with it all.

It turned out that he'd told Rich he'd met Kelly at a farm auction while on a buying trip for antiques. Kelly was astonished at his accuracy. St. Louis was, in fact, a center for antique dealing. Kelly had haunted the small-town auctions in search of antiques for years, furnishing not only her kitchen but dining room in handcrafted oak and walnut. But she'd never mentioned that to Matt.

By the time Rich left, Matt had painted an artful portrait of the common man. Positively reeking of authenticity, he'd shed insights into his fictitious life and career with such ease that the light of uncertainty had finally died in Rich's eyes. Rich even relaxed enough to laugh easily at some of Matt's more acerbic opinions, something he had a difficult time doing with anyone.

As an observer, Kelly was even more impressed than she was relieved. As a participant, she remained uneasy. Matt left no questions in his performance as to his relationship with her. He was solicitous and smiling, reaching over constantly to touch her hand, or just watch her talk. He played the caring, globetrotting lover who delighted in popping in to surprise her when he could. He'd taken her to the theater, the symphony and every Italian restaurant in town. And he highly approved that when he was away Kelly should enjoy Rich's company, because he liked Rich. Kelly, however, had the uncomfortable feeling that these fabrications were being painted a bit too broadly to be easily dispelled later when explanations would be in order.

And every time Matt looked at her with loving

eyes, she could feel his warmth reach her like a caress. It unsettled her even more.

Twenty minutes later when he reached the front door, Rich turned to shake Matt's hand and drop a tentative kiss on Kelly's forehead.

"Thanks for stopping by, Rich," she smiled warmly, still uncomfortable with the unconscious injustice she'd done him by comparing him to Matt. "I'll be back at work on Tuesday. See you then?"

He nodded, his eyes straying to Matt's easy smile, only briefly, before he guided his bike back out the door.

Matt waited a moment before turning to Kelly, his arm still comfortably around her shoulders. "Can you cook any better than you can make coffee?"

She shook her head, his proximity suddenly unsettling. "Hot dogs and peanut butter sandwiches. Michael was the cook."

It had, after all, been his job, his life and his abiding passion. Kelly had gained twenty pounds the first year they'd been married, and lost thirty after he'd died.

The thought of Michael made Matt's touch burn. Kelly shirked it awkwardly and walked over to put away the knitting bag she had carried to work.

"You have a number of questions to answer, Mr. Matthews." Her voice echoed accusingly from the back of the hall closet where she bent.

"You're great at improvs, you know that?"

Kelly straightened, facing his easy smile. "What?"

"Improvisations. You're a natural."

"That's one of the answers I want." She sounded angry and realized that now that she was alone with Matt Hennessy, a knot was beginning to form in her chest. Her life, so carefully structured and jealously closed since Michael's death, was threatened with chaos. The control she'd so painstakingly reconstructed had depended on the reliability of daily routine. It had become her life as well as her job to put things into logical order and to rearrange the pieces into something easily recognizable. Her ordered world suddenly seemed in danger before the onslaught of this glib man who'd swept in and taken it all completely out of her hands.

It wasn't that she couldn't empathize with him. She just wished he had picked someone else to help him protect his secret identity.

Maybe she shouldn't have taken that chance after all. Perhaps she should throw him out now before his confident, self-serving dynamism ran roughshod over her precarious hold on survival. Before his electric eyes and gentle hands began to haunt her.

"How about getting your answers over Sunday brunch?" he said grinning. "Restaurant of your choice."

"It *is* the least I deserve," she said, eyeing him suspiciously. "Yesterday you were running from the crowds. You want more?"

He smiled brightly, hands outstretched. "I court danger for a living."

"You just don't want hot dogs for breakfast. Do you promise not to pop any more surprises on me until the rest is explained?"

His hand went dramatically to his heart. "On my honor as an Eagle Scout."

An answering grin tugged reluctantly at the corners of her mouth. "Is that Paul Matthews, Matt Hennessy, or someone I haven't been introduced to yet, speaking?"

The restaurant Kelly settled on was a small storefront cafe that had been converted from an old greasy spoon into a woodwork-framed eatery of some distinction. The food was plentiful and varied, the clientele upper-middle-class professionals. Matt fit right in with the atmosphere, where lush plants vied for window space with soft sunlight, and corduroy jackets and monogrammed sweaters decorated the customers. Several people did hesitant double takes as Kelly and Matt walked to their window table, but no one betrayed frank recognition.

"See?" Matt smiled as he held a chair for her, a Swedish ivy plant framing his dark hair as he bent below a planter. "It can be done."

"Until they see the newspapers," she countered. "Your picture's spread across the magazine section like the most wanted man. No pun intended."

He grinned. Sunlight warmed his tanned skin and skittered across the shifting colors of his eyes in a way that made them seem almost unreal. It made his dark good looks appear even more striking—a countenance that could master frightening rage or melt with loss. Kelly had seen him do it on-screen and couldn't help but wonder just a little at the legitimacy of the gratitude that lit his eyes as he faced her.

Before Matt could speak, a waitress arrived, quickly rattling off menu items as she took the time to openly appreciate Matt's good looks. She had obviously not seen the paper yet either. Her easy patter was uninhibited and impersonal and her blonde smile was calculated to impress any handsome man. Kelly saw the tension ease in Matt's shoulders and wondered what it must be like to always be poised for escape.

"Why didn't you tell me the truth?" she asked after

they were served. "You had several opportunities, you know."

He gave an off-handed shrug. "I don't know. I guess that I wanted to spend a little time incognito. I was enjoying your company so much that I didn't want to take a chance that you'd...change when you found out just who I was."

"That's usually what happens?"

He nodded. "That's usually what happens. It gets really hard after a while when you can't even go to the store or a gas station without being under a magnifying glass. Everyone expects me to be the perfect, witty gentleman whose skin is as clear as his reputation." He looked up from his thoughts. "People sometimes fantasize they're Matt Hennessy. Well, sometimes I fantasize I'm them. You have to admit that you weren't as tense last night as you are now."

Kelly took a sip of coffee and nodded. "Last night I didn't know I was harboring a fugitive from international notoriety. Finding out was not the high point of my day."

Matt considered her lightly. "Did you really mind?"

It didn't take her long to answer. "Yes, I did." She remembered the heart-stopping shock at recognizing the picture. "I don't like surprises. But what I really don't like is people playing head games with my friends without their knowledge or consent. I'm not really thrilled by the prospect of explaining my part in all this to Rich once you catch the bus back to Wonderland."

"Oh, Rich is a nice guy," he assured her with a blithe wave of his coffee cup. "He'll understand."

She realized that over twenty-four hours without appreciable sleep did little for her patience. "And just what if he doesn't?" she demanded, leaning forward a little.

Matt looked up in surprise, his eyes wide. "You're not planning to marry him or anything, are you?"

Kelly's food was getting cold as she stared at Matt slack-jawed.

"Just what business is it of yours?"

Matt set his own fork down. "Don't get me wrong. I liked Rich a lot. I just didn't get the impression that you two were serious. He seemed too...conventional for you, Kel. You need more spontaneity in your life." He grinned mischievously. "Like me. More stray puppies."

"Do me a favor?" she asked brittlely. "Don't give me any help. Believe it or not, I've been doing pretty well without it so far, and I think I can manage to limp on through the future all by myself."

He never flinched before a glare that had shattered belligerent patients like cheap glass. "What's wrong with an unbiased opinion? People in L.A. pay for that kind of thing all the time."

Kelly was just tired and upset enough to have trouble knowing whether he was serious or not. "People in St. Louis consider it butting in," she retorted. "Just what do you think this is, anyway—a Cary Grant movie where you arrive just in time to save the befuddled heroine with a few well-chosen words?"

Matt scowled handsomely. "See what I mean? You need some surprises in your life. You're probably lucky that I came along when I did. I think I'm saving you from a life of boredom."

She'd been glaring at the twinkle in his eyes all along and had squared off eyeball- to-eyeball at his outrageous self-confidence. It had been all she could do to sit still for it, uncertain whether he could possibly be that shallow and blithely unfair. She wanted to either set him straight with dispatch or discover some other truth beneath the incessant goading.

But suddenly as she opened her mouth to offer a particularly biting retort, she saw him as a picture. The picture of Matt Hennessy, film star, raconteur, polo player. Matt Hennessy, whom she was chastising like a recalcitrant five-year-old child.

And just as suddenly, she lost her words. A sense of unreality engulfed her, smothering her with its almost hallucinatory feeling of absurdity. How had she ended up here? What was she doing talking to the man she and countless other women had fantasized about, as if she'd known him all her life? What had happened to the carefully measured safety of her life?

Abruptly pushing her food away, Kelly stood.

"Uh, excuse me..." She faltered, turned to escape.

The waitress passed her with a new pot of coffee, her makeup freshened and her eye on Matt. Kelly wanted to laugh. The girl still had no idea who she was ogling. She just thought Matt was an attractive man. If she'd known who he really was, she would have been a quivering mass of Jell-O. Kelly just couldn't deal with it.

Without another word, she fled to the quiet of the ladies room. She had to get somewhere Matt couldn't follow.

She found a small chair beneath the hand dryer, and sank gratefully into it, trembling a little. For a few long moments, she wasn't at all sure that she could go back out there. Too much had happened on too little sleep, and she was afraid she was beginning to lose control. And not with ordinary pressures like bills or washing machines breaking or reminders of Michael popping up at vulnerable moments. She'd been tossed straight into *The Twilight Zone.*

Kelly had stepped into a fantasy millions of women would willingly sell their children to have, and suddenly she wasn't all that sure she wanted any part of it. Matt Hennessy belonged in a different orbit than she. He was a mover, a shaker, a man who courted legends and consorted with immortality. He had talent that most people dreamed of and envied in equal proportions. Kelly was a good nurse who considered a visit to a local shopping center a big night out. Matt Hennessy simply didn't fit into her life.

Kelly sat and stared disconsolately at her reflection in the mirror. Dark circles accented her bloodshot blue eyes, and the makeup she'd slapped on the night before had never seen reinforcements. Her lips looked as if someone had been siphoning at her neck, and her hair was beginning to slide untidily out of its topknot.

Kelly did laugh then, a shrill, silly sound that echoed hollowly off the green-and-white tile walls. The thought that Matt Hennessy had actually kissed the underweight phantom she faced was too ludicrous to believe, even if it had only been a game.

The blue eyes in the mirror sparkled a bit. A game. Only a game. That was how Matt treated the situation, so maybe she should feel the same. He'd taken her to breakfast to thank her for her hospitality, and then he'd vanish again into a puff of blue smoke, letting her get on with her life. Sometime when he was on television, he might mention a funny incident of how he'd escaped the St. Louis press by jumping into some strange young woman's car. And Kelly would have to repeat the story, at Missy's insistence for any people who didn't know. She could surely afford one more hour out of her life without disrupting it too much.

When Kelly returned to the table, Matt stood to greet her with solicitous eyes.

"Are you all right?"

She smiled as she slid back into the booth. "I'm fine." A voice way inside her wanted to know how she could be so flustered one minute and so calm the next. Training, she told herself. A good emergency nurse should be able to stay calm in the face of anything. Still, the sense of unreality persisted. "I just overwhelm a bit more easily after a sleepless night."

"Overwhelm?"

Her smile broadened. "I had more than my allowed number of shocks and upsets before breakfast today. I have to admit to some tension."

"Well, pretend I'm Paul Matthews again," he suggested playfully. "We seemed to get along pretty well then."

Kelly shook her head, returning her attention to the food she'd earlier deserted. Matt was already on his coffee. "Too late. It's okay, I just did what I always do with people who make me nervous."

"What's that?"

"Well," she said, neatly dispatching some eggs and going for the ham, "I usually picture people in their underwear. It makes them seem more human. Unfortunately in your case, it just made me more nervous."

He grimaced painfully.

Kelly found that this time when she looked at him, she felt more settled, a little more in control. "I can't help it if you're built like a fantasy of mine. I decided instead to picture you with a crow sitting on your head."

Matt stared, not exactly sure how to react.

Kelly laughed, much more relaxed. "You know, that's exactly how I pictured you."

"So," Matt spoke up a moment later. "You're a nurse. Rich said that you work in the emergency room."

Kelly looked up and gave him a wry smile. "Only when I can't find any strange men to lure into my car."

He grinned easily. "I've never known an emergency room nurse before."

Kelly looked back at him lazily, leaning forward a little for emphasis. "Is this where I'm supposed to say, 'Gee, I've never known a movie star before?'"

Matt chuckled, his eyes bright with pleasure. "You sure regain your equilibrium fast."

"It's all in the wrists." She chuckled at the amusement in Matt's eyes. It amazed her that his smile could send a shiver creeping up her legs. No wonder this guy was everybody's fantasy. He deserved it. Trying to ease the pressure his bright smile was causing, Kelly decided to move on to a new topic. "So, what are you doing in St. Louis? It's not exactly the beaten track for movie idols with time on their hands."

Matt paused as he stirred absently at his coffee, his eyes mischievous. "Why should I tell you?"

"Somewhere at the top of the list is the fact that I didn't squeal on you when you were doing your Paul Matthews impersonation."

"I told you," he countered blithely, "you enjoyed every minute of it. Your life could do with more improvs and surprises. Opens your horizons."

"Damn it," she accused, setting her coffee cup down just a bit too hard. "You're doing it again. Do you think that just because I live in a Midwest city and work a regular job that my life has no meaning? This may come as a surprise to you, but I haven't been

waiting my whole life for you to turn my lackluster existence into magic. I think you'd better stop reading
your press releases, pal. You're beginning to believe
them!"

"Meredith Mason."

He'd brought her up short in the midst of her indignation. She blinked. "What?"

He smiled at her, leaning toward her over the pol-
ished butcher-block table. "That's why I'm in St. Louis.
Meredith and I are...an item. I stopped by to surprise
her."

"Yeah, I've heard the story. Meredith Mason, huh?"

He grinned at her reaction. "Yep. Mismatch of the
century."

That was a conservative description. Meredith
Mason currently reigned as the first lady of American
theater. The ice queen herself. Blonde, cultured, statuesque, rigidly private and an indisputable legend,
she considered it beneath her to sully her reputation
by even saying the word Hollywood. And here she was
dating its premier beefcake. Wouldn't the tabloids just
die to know that Matt Hennessy had made a special
trip to St. Louis to see her while she appeared in the
Tennessee Williams tribute. It would be like Helen of
Troy meeting Hercules.

For the briefest of moments, Kelly remembered
the astonishing fire Matt's kisses had ignited in her,
and she found herself caught by the unmistakable tug
of jealousy. She immediately dismissed it.

"You have good taste," she said, her eyes wide.
"You two will be all the rage."

He scowled. "We've managed a fair amount of
anonymity up to now."

Kelly grinned knowingly. "Well good luck, my
friend, 'cause the minute anybody sees you in St.

Louis, they're going to put two and two together real fast."

They'd gotten all the way to the front to pay the bill before someone saw the paper.

"Oh, my God!" It was a stage whisper, a turned head. Then more whispering, urgent, excited.

Kelly saw it first. "I think you've just been unmasked, Batman."

Matt looked up to see the first fan tentatively approach. The woman, untidily plump and nudging middle age, smiled like a car dealer. She never even knew Kelly was there.

"You're Matt Hennessy, aren't you?" she asked, blocking Matt's escape.

When Matt turned to answer, Kelly couldn't believe the change in him. The only word she could think of to describe it was gloss. His eyes and teeth sparkled, he smiled just enough to produce the famous dimples. Gracious with the proper modicum of modesty, he murmured melodiously over the woman's enthusiasm.

Within minutes, the crowd had descended, anxiously reaching for Matt's hand, their eyes memorizing every moment. Matt handled them deftly, easing his way over to the door as he signed napkins and traded banalities with people who, ten minutes earlier, had considered themselves above simpering. Even the waitress, suddenly a pile of Jell-O as Kelly had predicted, tailed Matt with something that resembled the diligent adoration of a spaniel.

Kelly edged along the windows, thankful that she was too small to have to dodge plant hangers, and made it to the car by the time Matt had backed out of the restaurant. She was moving even before he had a chance to close the car door. A few people tried to follow, but she knew Webster well. There was a wealth of back streets to get lost on before hitting the highway.

"Would you like a job as a chauffeur?" Matt yelled, hanging on to the side of the car as Kelly made a sharp turn into the fast lane.

She grinned, her adrenaline level high. "You couldn't afford my insurance."

"I believe that."

"That was a pretty impressive performance back there."

"Lots of practice."

He didn't sound terribly enthused. She could hardly blame him. It occurred to her that she would have acted the same way everyone else did if she'd recognized him in a public place, and that every restaurant must be like that.

Following his directions, Kelly pulled up before Matt's hotel and turned off the engine. He turned to face her.

"You've been a good sport, Kelly."

Her smile was a little shaky. "I know."

He reached out to take her hand. Kelly fought the exhilaration of his touch.

He smiled. "Sometime when you're out in L.A., you're going to have to let me return the hospitality."

Kelly tilted her head. "Does that include playing charades with your friends, or just poking fun at your lifestyle?"

He winced. "Not much thanks for all your help, was it?"

"That's okay," she said, smiling sincerely. "I haven't ever known a movie star before. You really weren't all that bad for my first."

When he smiled this time, he reached over to cup her chin in his hand, his eyes more serious than his voice. "And for my first episode of leaping into a beautiful woman's car, I was incredibly lucky. Thank you, Kelly."

Her own smile was off-hand even as she struggled to be free of his gaze. "Anytime, Paul."

He bent quickly to kiss her, his eyes bemused, and turned to leave. Kelly didn't move, the feel of his lips still vivid, his touch marking her uncomfortably. She saw him wave as he walked in the door, but couldn't move to return the gesture. She was suddenly tired and irritable, and she had to get home to resume her life.

But for a long moment, she continued to look at the door...and couldn't leave.

CHAPTER 3

T he first two things Kelly did when she woke up later that afternoon were to turn her phone back on and feed Fritz. Fritz was the neighborhood cat, a complacent old tabby that made the rounds for his meals and affection without objections from any of his benefactors. Today seemed to be Kelly's day on his schedule, and he was quite annoyed that she hadn't fulfilled her duties more promptly.

He was even more upset when, in the middle of dishing out his food, Kelly had to answer the phone. Stalking over to stand obstinately between her legs, he beat a rhythm against her calf with his switching tail.

"Knock it off, you old rogue," she said, grinning at him, the receiver already almost at her ear. "Hello?"

"Who's a rogue? Is it him? Damn it, Kelly, what have you two been doing all day? I've been trying to get you since noon! Tell me all about it, girl. And then invite me over. I'm at least polite enough to ask to be invited."

"Missy, what are you babbling about? I don't know what Fritz has been doing all day, but I've been asleep. I turned off the phone."

"Asleep? Are you crazy?"

Kelly tried to get away from Fritz without success. His tail beat all the harder. "Missy, you are absolutely foaming at the mouth. Try and be a bit more lucid, will you?"

Kelly heard the sigh on the other end, as if Missy were finding the patience to deal with a slow child or a bad liar. She could almost see her friend roll her eloquent brown eyes in exasperation.

"How long have we been friends, Kelly? Haven't I gone through thick and thin with you?"

"Thick and thin. Get to the point, Missy. Fritz is waiting to eat."

"And I've been waiting all my life to meet someone like Matt Hennessy."

Kelly knew that if her jaw hadn't been attached, it would have shattered on the linoleum. "Oh."

"Oh? Oh! A little anticlimactic, aren't we? I don't want 'oh.' I want details. And I want to know why the hell you didn't tell your best friend this morning."

She didn't even feel Fritz's impatient attacks anymore. "How did you find out?"

"The morning news. Jenny called me. She saw a film of Matt Hennessy jumping into *your* car."

"The news? Oh, no."

"Well," Missy chastised, "you couldn't keep it a secret for long...even though, God knows you tried. You didn't even tell me!"

"Missy, I didn't know!" Fritz made one more try to get Kelly's attention and then hopped to the counter to eat from the can. Any other time, Kelly would have clobbered him.

"You didn't know?" Skepticism dripped heavily from Missy's voice.

"I believe you said something about Superman

and glasses this morning. That's just what happened to me. I didn't know who he was."

Knowing that there was no way out of it, she gave Missy the pertinent details.

She got as far as the morning scene they'd played for Rich's benefit, at which point she was sure Missy had dropped the phone.

"Matt Hennessy kissed you?"

"And I'm still alive," Kelly retorted dryly. Yet all of a sudden she was breathless with the memory.

"Well, we could at least cut up the sheets he slept on and sell them for souvenirs."

"Really crass, Miss."

"All right then, when's he coming to see you again? Will you call me or should I just camp out on your porch?"

Kelly sighed. "He's not. He's gone back to being Matt Hennessy, and my coachmen are mice again."

There was a pause. When Kelly heard Missy's voice, it was quieter. "Well, I think I'll come by later anyway. We'll both be awake for a while, and *Gunga Din's* on."

Kelly smiled, glad Missy was her friend. "That sounds great, Miss. I'll see you then."

She hung up the phone and finally noticed Fritz, who'd just about finished his lunch. He turned to glare at her, his tail switching as if daring her to get mad. Grinning at his audacity, she let him stay where he was.

As she began to get dinner together for herself, Kelly couldn't help but reflect on the excitement of the past twenty-four hours. Thinking back, she had to admit that she was glad for the "moment of fantasy" she'd had. It was as if her fairy godmother had granted her twelve hours with the reigning movie king, and she had been able to handle it with some grace.

With one small exception, she'd talked to him without stuttering or going dumb. He'd kissed her twice, even in fun, and she'd twice had the chance to rescue him. Kelly was just glad it hadn't lasted any longer. She could still feel that shock of regret that had surprised her when he'd disappeared into the hotel.

Again, the phone interrupted her. She ignored it until she'd finished her own dinner and shooed Fritz back outside. By then the phone had rung three times.

"Miss Byrne, I'm from the news department at KSTV. Can you give me any information about your relationship with Matt Hennessy?"

Kelly sighed. "I gave him some help getting away from some reporters he didn't want to see, that's all. Good-bye."

The next four calls were identical. The fifth set her teeth on edge. She'd just given the reporter the same line when he interrupted her.

"Excuse me, ma'am, but we got hold of Mr. Hennessy a few minutes ago, and he admits to a long-standing relationship with you. He said that the two of you met at an antique auction and have been seeing each other regularly since. What we were hoping for was a live mini-cam interview for the six o'clock news. Just a filler. I could have someone over there in about fifteen minutes."

He seemed disconcerted when she didn't answer.

"Miss Byrne?"

The doorbell rang, breaking into Kelly's open-mouthed silence. She jumped, turning to it as if for explanation.

"Miss Byrne, are you there?"

"Uh, yes. Yes, I am. And no, don't come to my house unless you want your mini-cam in pieces. In about as many pieces as Mr. Hennessy is going to find his jaw," she added beneath her breath.

She hung up as the doorbell sounded again in insistent jabs. What was Missy doing here already? It usually took her a good hour just to get her makeup on. Then a new thought struck Kelly, and she looked down at the phone, startled. What if it wasn't Missy? What if it was more reporters? Maybe they were here to cover whatever story Matt had been dishing out to them.

She snuck to the window for a peak. No camera truck. No Missy, either. A nondescript sedan sat in the driveway. Kelly thought she saw someone in the passenger's seat.

"Who is it?" she finally asked, ready to chase any reporters away.

"Kelly, I have to talk to you!"

She couldn't stand much more of this. Angrily, she threw the door open. Matt stood before her, his casual clothes exchanged for a dark suit, his face clean shaven and shining. He smiled a bit apologetically, and dimples creased his cheeks.

"I suppose you're here so the live mini-cam can get film for our long-standing relationship!" Kelly howled.

"Kelly..."

"Don't Kelly me! Just who do you think you are? Do I have a sign on my back that says Kick Me?"

His eyes remained patient. "Kelly, you're causing a scene. Let me come in and explain."

"Not on your life, you asshole. Go away and leave me alone."

"But you have to understand." He stood in the light, ignoring the moths that fluttered against him.

Kelly knew her voice carried, and it suddenly dawned on her that her neighbors had all probably seen the news, too. They were simply too polite to come over and demand explanations. They would, however, wait at their windows for scene two, which she was now giving them in stereo.

"Get in here," she growled and turned on her heel.

Matt followed, standing silently by as she gathered her badly frayed wits about her.

"Do you know that when you're mad you're—"

She whipped around, a warning finger poised. "Don't."

He grinned. "Well, you're beautiful, too. But you can be a little hellcat if you want."

"I'm not even wound up yet," she warned blackly. "Just wait till the next reporter calls."

"That's what I wanted to talk to you about." He motioned to the couch. "Can we sit down?"

Kelly stalked over to a wing chair and sat. It occurred to her briefly that Matt was once again seeing her at her worst. Although she felt better after six hours of sleep, she hadn't yet had a chance to shower. She was in jeans and an old work shirt of Michael's that was tied at the waist, and her as yet unwashed hair was pulled into a ponytail that hung limply down her back.

Matt looked as if he'd stepped out of an ad for Dom Perignon. He sat on the edge of the couch and leaned forward, his hands together, his elbows on his knees. The picture of concern. Kelly wondered who he was playing this time.

"I've been trying to get hold of you for hours," he began, his voice sounding earnest.

She sat stiffly, not giving him any encouragement. "I was asleep. I turn my phone off when I sleep."

"I wanted to ask what you thought of the idea first, but then the news crews found me—"

"You're going to have to stop dropping bread crumbs."

He should have been insulted. Instead, he grinned. "It's the perfect plan, if you'll help."

"What is?"

As if needing to give motion to his ideas, he stood and crossed the room to the fireplace before turning back to face her, his face animated. "My cover for being in St. Louis," he said. "A way to keep the vultures from Meredith."

"By dropping them on me?"

He walked over to her, and again Kelly was struck by his physical presence. The base of her scalp tingled as he neared, and when he sat in the other chair to face her she unconsciously moved back. That electrical field of his tended to sap her resolve.

"I'll make you a deal," he offered, leaning forward again. "Be my leading lady for two weeks, and I'll take you to the finest restaurants, get you first row seats at the theater, anything you want. I'll fly you to any city just for dinner. If you and I can make a splash, they'd leave Meredith and me alone."

"If you spend all this time with me, when would you see Meredith?"

His grin broadened in delight over her apparent impending capitulation. "Anytime but when she's at the theater. I'd be with you then."

She refused to look at him. "All for the low price of letting the press hound me every waking minute for the next six months or so."

"That was bound to happen the minute they got that film of you driving off with me. After what I've seen of you in the past two days, though, I think you'd be able to handle the press just fine. God knows you keep me in my place."

"There are times when I think that requires a whip and a chair." She did look at him now with an appraising eye. "One thing I have to say for you, you really memorize the script before you do the scene."

He laughed, sounding relieved. "Just think of it as a trip to Fantasy Island. Wouldn't you really like to spend a couple of weeks rubbing elbows with the cream of society? Think about it, you'd have a great time. You pick the places, and I'll take you there. I'll be the perfect gentleman, and the only demands made on you would be the press attention, which you already have. It'll be just like a game. Like playing a game, Kel."

She would have had to have been nuts or dead an hour not to react to his offer. Who wouldn't love to be seen on the arm of Matt Hennessy? He was handsome, funny, attentive—the ultimate fantasy man. She could float around in the rarefied atmosphere of wealth she'd only heard of, acting the part of Cinderella. Dinner at Tony's, Busch's Grove, Port St. Louis. Lunch at the Pump Room in Chicago or Galatoire's in New Orleans, dinner at 21 in New York if she really wanted. And all on the very eligible arm of Matt Hennessy. Kelly had always had a secret desire to be enviable, and that would do it in spades.

And when midnight came, she'd just turn in her glass slippers and go back to being Kelly Byrne, whose life was destined to the quiet streets and hospital hallways of the St. Louis suburbs.

When it was over, she'd have to return home to a house made empty by Michael's death, and even more empty by the flash of time Matt had been there. She'd have to return to being alone, something she'd just begun to be comfortable with again. The silence in her life would become louder, its prison stronger.

Kelly looked up at the animation in Matt's eyes, at the strong handsome planes of his face, the curl of his mouth. She thought of the brief moments when he'd aroused her, even in charade, and it brought her new pain.

And then she remembered what he'd already told the press without benefit of consulting her. It was as if her opinion was assured or didn't matter. Could he really be that insensitive? He'd spent the past four years being waited on hand and foot, his every wish met before he made it. The singularity of that attention and adulation would affect anyone, and Kelly had no idea just how well-founded his "good guy" image was to begin with. She'd seen him handle a crowd like a faith healer. Maybe it was harder to dazzle the press, but she had no doubts that this man could do it. He was a glamorous, handsome, charismatic man who'd been taught self-absorption by the world he inherited with his stardom. Was that really something Kelly wanted to become involved with? Did she really want to taste his world and then be left with her own?

"No," she said simply, getting to her feet.

Matt's face fell into incredulity. "Kelly, think about it."

"I haven't been in a trance, Matt. The answer is no. It's too improbable. I don't think it'd work, and if I were Meredith, I don't think I'd like it a bit."

"She loved the idea," he insisted, standing and approaching her. "Meredith's a maniac about her privacy, and I've been a serious threat to it. This seemed a good way to throw the hounds off the scent."

"Is this something you're planning everywhere you two travel together, or just the Midwest?"

"Just here," he said. "One performance only. Meredith has already told me that she'd rather I didn't surprise her again."

The look Kelly gave him left no doubt as to how she, too, felt on the subject. "Hire an actress to play my part," she suggested dryly. "One who looks more appropriate."

He stood before her now, looking down at the top of her head. She stood with her legs against the chair, nowhere to escape. Again the nape of her neck warned of his proximity. She felt as if a strange heat were seeping through her, down to her very limbs, where it seemed to enervate her.

"More appropriate than what?" he asked, his voice like music. A convincing recitative, the lilt concerned and sincere.

Kelly grinned ruefully, throwing her arms out for inspection. "We have to consider credibility here, you know. Who in their right mind would single me out as the latest hot affair of Matt Hennessy?"

Matt cupped her chin with two fingers and raised it so that she would have to face the quiet amusement in his eyes. "Don't sell yourself short, Kelly. If you hadn't been just who you were, I would have jumped right back out of your car and kept on running."

The sincerity in his green eyes held her so that it was a moment before she could manage an answer. "I doubt it," she said, her voice a little too quiet. "You would have driven off with Darth Vader if he'd had a fast car."

Now she saw a flash of consternation touch those eyes, and she felt his hand tense. She hadn't been able to pull from his touch even though it began to sear through her.

"Didn't that husband of yours ever tell you how beautiful you are?" he demanded.

That stiffened her. Abruptly she pulled away from him, glaring at his presumption. "Sometimes you have the sensitivity of a jackhammer, you know it? You can't walk in and take over my life like it was your God-given right. I said no once and I meant it, Matt. You're a lot of fun, but I can't transform the next two weeks of my life just to suit you. It doesn't work that way." She refused to soften beneath the challenge her words set off in him. "That leaves it up to you to explain to the press how it was a case of mistaken identity, and that you never met me before yesterday."

As if on cue, the phone rang. They both turned to it. "And you can start right now."

Pushing him out of the way, Kelly stalked over to the offending instrument, picked it up and handed it to him. She should have known better.

With a triumphant grin, Matt took hold of the phone and greeted the caller effusively. "Yes, this is...oh yes, it's quite true. I got into town yesterday and hope to see Kelly as her schedule permits over the next two weeks..."

"Hey, wait!" Kelly protested, grabbing for the phone. "Don't do that! Damn it, I told you no!"

It was no trick at all to keep the phone out of reach. Matt ignored her.

"No, I'm just leaving now. I'd consider it a personal favor if you wouldn't bother Kelly. We'll talk to you at the opening on Friday, and I'm sure we'll see you around town...yes, thanks...yeah, you too. Good-bye."

Kelly was incensed. He'd just done it again, just as if she hadn't spent the past five minutes explaining why he couldn't.

"Don't you ever consider anyone but yourself?"

she demanded, hands on hips. "I am not—repeat *not* —going out with you. And the more you insist, the more obstinate I'll become. I have no intention of playing your game, Mr. Hennessy. End of discussion."

Without warning, he caught her by the arms and pulled her to him. She didn't even have a chance to object. She'd raised her head to challenge him face to face, her lips opened to initiate protest. He caught her there, his mouth trapping hers, the force of his kiss bending her head back. She couldn't breathe, couldn't move against him. Kelly fought against the reaction she knew would come. Fought and lost. Within the span of a heartbeat she dissolved, folding into the hard planes of his body as if poured there.

Just as suddenly, he pulled away, his face close, his eyes incredibly gentle as they searched Kelly's. "Ever see *Honky Tonk*, Kelly? Let me give you some real Clark Gable advice. 'Jump in and get wet all at once. You'll feel great.'" Dropping another quick kiss on her lips, he straightened to leave. "I don't want you to do it for me, Kelly. I want you to do it for you. I'll call tomorrow."

~

IT SEEMED ONLY a few minutes before Missy was pounding on the door. Kelly started as if physically struck. She hadn't moved from where Matt had left her.

Missy didn't take the time to wait for an answer, and before Kelly could get over to the door, the tall blonde swept in, an unnatural fire burning in her carefully made-up eyes.

"No, Missy, Matt Hennessy won't be over," she mimicked dryly, hands on hips. "It's a good thing I don't trust you, or I would have missed him completely. Again."

Kelly looked at her friend, her own expression blank. "He surprised me again."

Missy laughed. "Surprised the hell out of me, too. I thought he was Rich." As if by mutual consent, they both headed for the kitchen. "Kelly, he is so sweet. He stopped and talked to me as if he'd known me all his life...well, he had to. I'd blocked his car. Almost ran right over him when I saw who it was. And you're not going to believe who I could have sworn was in the car with him."

"Meredith Mason."

Missy stopped dead in her tracks for just a moment, as much from Kelly's tone of voice as from her answer. "You're right. Hey, kid, what's the matter? You look strangely subdued for someone who's just spent time with the most handsome man in America. Of course, I'd be depressed too if he caught me looking like a punk house painter." There was a minute pause as Missy pulled out a soda and let her mind shift gears. "How did you know that that was Meredith Mason? Meredith Mason, for God's sake. What a story! What's the *Enquirer's* phone number?"

Kelly grinned, now even more glad that Missy had decided to come over. Her manic common sense had seen Kelly through some really rough days, and Kelly was thankful for it.

Missy was four years or so Kelly's junior. They'd met at work the day Missy had transferred to the emergency room and set the place on its ear. She was the Jeff to Kelly's Mutt, standing a statuesque five-eleven with what Missy called "chosen" honey-blonde hair and dark brown eyes. Missy was always meticulously groomed, even down to the contraband red nail polish she wore at work; she prided herself on finding a new love at least once a week and tirelessly mothered Kelly and any other of her friends who needed it. Enjoying her company was just a matter of sifting through her rapid-fire sentences for pertinent facts. Kelly had become something of an expert on it.

"Just which question do you want answered?" she asked, getting out the popcorn popper and beginning to feel the reality of her everyday life seep back in.

"All of them, of course. But especially why you look like somebody just shot your pet goat."

"Let's sit down, and I'll explain it all over *Gunga Din*," Kelly suggested. "And do me a favor. Go out and turn off the phone."

Missy looked at her a moment with bemused eyes, shrugged, and walked out.

By the time Kelly had finished explaining not only the situation but what she considered to be her perfectly legitimate reaction to it, they'd missed half of the movie. Missy's outrage took up the other half.

"Are you crazy?" she demanded, spilling popcorn onto the rug in front of her. "Are you out of your mind? Don't you know what he's offering?"

"Sure," Kelly retorted dryly, her eyes on the TV, "the moon, the stars, all this and heaven, too. Isn't that how it goes? I'm just not the kind of person to run off for two weeks of Disneyland without waiting for the penance. There's a piper out there somewhere to be paid."

"Oh for heaven's sake, girl, I just don't believe you. You're talking like you'd be spending two weeks at the dentist. This is Matt Hennessy you're talking about. He's offering to fulfill every fantasy—well, almost every fantasy—with no strings attached and, if you ask me, you could really use that right now. Nobody in her right mind would turn down a chance like that. Two weeks with Matt Hennessy? Honey, if I had the chance, by the end of that time, he'd either forget what the words Meredith Mason meant or he'd be dead from exhaustion. If I believed that you were really as disinterested as you're acting, I'd consign you to a shrink."

Kelly turned from the groveling eyes of Sam Jaffee to Missy's incredulity. Popcorn fell, bouncing over Kelly. Missy was really getting worked up. "I'm glad you see it my way, Missy. It makes it so much easier when I don't have to defend motives. Or explain that it's still too early for me to stand the hassle of...*consorting* with someone like Matt Hennessy."

"That's just the point. You wouldn't be involved. You'd stay friends, like with Rich...only more fun."

"Missy."

"Don't get me wrong, Kelly. I like Rich a lot. But he's about as exciting as hernia surgery."

For the first time that day, Kelly laughed, letting her tensions ease out a little. "I appreciate the concern, Missy. But I don't need excitement right now. I need stability."

"Bullshit. You're smothering in stability. You're turning into an old widow woman before my very eyes. What you need is to do up that mass of hair and sprinkle it with diamonds. Get a dress from Neiman-Marcus that would set Bill Blass gasping, and let me teach you how to bring out those eyes of yours. Do you know that I'd kill for eyes like that? Blue eyes and naturally black lashes, and you don't even use eye shadow. I could die. Then you need to be unleashed on a roomful of socialites while you're on the arm of Matt Hennessy, and you'd cause shock waves all the way to New York. That's what you need."

Kelly dismissed the words with a wave of her hand. Cary Grant was about to be a hero, and she didn't want to miss it. Gunfire sputtered from the set as shoe-polished extras fought the Queen's finest. This was the kind of escapism Kelly enjoyed. She'd never met Cary Grant and couldn't be disillusioned.

Missy actually held off until the end of the movie and the reading of the famous poem in tribute to Sam Jaffee's acting ability to continue her argument.

"Just think," she said laconically. "He was reincarnated as the High Lama of Shangri La. You're going with Matt to that opening."

"I am not. I work this week."

"Somebody'll trade with you. After all, your honey's in town to see you. Everybody knows that."

Kelly sighed and picked up the overflow popcorn before she slowly got to her feet. "Missy, be a friend. Agree with me for once."

Missy stood with her, her face uncommonly serious. "No, Kelly. You haven't been alive since Michael died. Jump back in. You'll be surprised how much you'll like it."

Kelly couldn't keep the wry humor from her tired eyes. "Why do I have the feeling that if this weren't Matt Hennessy we were talking about, you wouldn't be quite so insistent."

Missy's grin was smug. "Because I wouldn't. A chance in a lifetime doesn't wander into town that often. I don't want to miss it."

"If you want to see him so badly, you go out with him."

Missy smiled again, and Kelly saw the determination there. "He doesn't want to go out with me—foolish man—he wants to go out with you."

For a brief moment, Kelly actually wondered

which would be worse in the long run, the reporters or Missy. She almost capitulated on the spot. Matt was bad enough and Missy was worse, but the two of them working together might very well be more than she could handle.

As she said good-night at the door, Kelly raised a warning finger. "Missy, I don't want to hear a word about this at work tomorrow. By then I'll have convinced Matt to leave me alone, and I can finally get my life back to normal."

Missy just laughed. "I don't know what you underestimate more, kid, Matt's power of persuasion or your power of attraction."

By five o'clock the next afternoon, Kelly discovered that she'd at least underestimated Matt's persistence.

CHAPTER 4

The day started out quietly enough. Kelly left the phone off the hook to avoid curious reporters, slept until nine and ate breakfast with the Today Show and a proponent for legalized marijuana. Since it was Monday, she did her weekly shopping and washed and waxed the floors before allowing herself a twenty-minute bath with a good book.

Work kept her loneliness at bay, and the book should have kept thoughts of Matt at bay. But as she soaked in the hot water, she remembered the delicious fire of his touch and the way his eyes held hers. Even as she realized that her decision was a sensible one, she felt unaccountably sad. It was as if she had lost something precious.

As always, she arrived at work at two-fifteen. The custom had originated in the days when she'd sought to escape the overwhelming emptiness of a suddenly silent house and had long since hardened into a comfortable ritual. She usually changed right away into the scrubs and lab coat she wore for work, and then settled into the nurses' lounge with a book and soda to pass the time until shift change at three.

Sometimes it occurred to her that the chaotic circus atmosphere of work had become more like home than home. It was a place she'd made her own. Nobody expected more or less of her than she could give. She felt comfortable no matter where she went in the hospital, and the companionship of her friends there provided a familiar salve to any trouble she found in the old house in Webster.

Not today.

Because of a thirty-second news clip on the news she'd been propelled into notoriety. Nobody ever expected to be touched by fame, no matter how second or third hand, and just about everybody greeted her with expectant eyes and breathless questions. Had she really saved Matt Hennessy? Was he as suave as he looked on the awards shows, or as tough as in the movies?

Seven nurses crowded into the bathroom with her while she struggled to get out of her jeans, and another ten waited in the lounge. Three of her friends who had known her a long time and well enough to know that she didn't have a long-standing relationship with anyone, much less Matt Hennessy—brought cameras just in case they could catch the happy couple for posterity. The Cinderella story, it seemed, was still popular.

To make the afternoon even more pleasant, the supervisor, an octogenarian nun with no sense of humor and even less patience, caught the budding riot in her lounge. With glacial dispatch, she ushered the culprits back out to work and delivered her verdict on Kelly's participation with one long, dour look. Kelly knew better than to attempt an explanation. Sister Agatha detested explanations. They seemed to waste the precious time she had to rule her small world.

The crowning blow, though, came at dinner, courtesy of Matt himself.

It was five o'clock. The day shift had finally given up and gone home, and in the past half hour only a handful of people had dropped in from other departments to inquire about the state of Kelly's love life. Kelly stood by the drug cabinet waiting for Missy to make it back from her station at the triage desk so the two of them could go to dinner.

When Missy did show up, the cat-in-the-cream smile on her face sent Kelly's stomach plummeting all over again.

"Better come out to the desk," she told Kelly.

Everyone went out to the desk.

A tall, dignified man stood rigidly by the outside door as if sculpted there. He stared straight ahead, chauffeur's cap held beneath one arm in military fashion. Outside in the garage, Kelly saw a block-long limo with smoke-tinted windows. The chauffeur and car seemed to belong to each other.

When Kelly approached with entourage in tow, the chauffeur unriveted his eyes from the far wall and turned to her with a crisp bow. She'd seen bows like that in World War II movies, and had to restrain a brief urge to bow back.

"Excuse me," he spoke up crisply, "are you Ms. Kelly Byrne?"

A Brooklyn accent. How out of character. Kelly nodded hesitantly, a great bubble of anxiety inflating in her chest. The chauffeur stepped to the side, and for the first time Kelly realized that another person stood behind him. Small, young, spare and very deferential, the man wore a well-cut suit and held on precariously to two very large boxes. One bore the

Neiman-Marcus label. Kelly groaned. A murmur rose from behind her.

The smaller man stepped forward and smiled. "These are for you, miss."

Smiling hesitantly, he handed over the other box, the unmarked one, and Kelly realized it was from a florist. So, it seemed, did everybody else.

The anxiety metamorphosed, suddenly resembled giddiness. Kelly found herself wanting to giggle. "Oh," she said, shaking her head with a straight face, deciding not to act responsible for what was going to happen. That would be the last thing she needed. "I don't think I'm *that* Kelly Byrne."

Missy interrupted with her usual tact. "Don't be stupid. She's thrilled. Thank you very much." And she grabbed the box before Kelly could protest.

The minute Missy opened it, a thick aroma filled the artificially ventilated air and sent Kelly's onlookers to gasping. Three dozen long-stemmed red roses lay nestled in clouds of tissue. The silly exhilaration grew. This was so outrageous. She'd never had anything like this happen to her before. Nobody she knew had, come to think of it. One thing she could say for Matt, though: when he coerced obstinate women, he did it with style. If only he wouldn't do it so publicly.

"Darling." Kelly turned at the sound of Missy's voice. A small card was held between two of her infamous red nails. Kelly made a grab for it and lost. "Darling—" Missy started again "—'Knew I'd find you here. Don't forget the opening Friday. We've been invited for a ride on the *Delta Queen*. Until then, all my love, Matt. P.S. Wear the other gift just for me.'"

Missy smiled. The crowd of nurses pressed closer, and Kelly had to once again quell the urge to laugh.

The little man was holding out the Neiman-Marcus box to her.

"Mr. Hennessy didn't want us to detain you. He knew that you'd be busy. So if I can give this to you, we'll not keep you any longer."

Kelly couldn't help it. "What if I don't?" she asked, very conscious of her audience.

Several people gasped.

The little man's forehead crinkled above his bright little eyes, "Then I'm afraid we couldn't leave. Mr. Hennessy specifically told us not to leave until you accepted all three gifts."

"Of course he did," Kelly smiled dryly.

"Three?" Missy demanded hungrily.

The man nodded, whereupon Missy quite deftly relieved him of the Neiman-Marcus box so that he could pull out yet another. A small, square black velvet number that set the crowd on its ear.

Kelly stared at the bribes, the thrill of surprise beginning to share time with a building irritation. This was all getting a little heavy-handed. "There's a message I'd like you to give Mr. Hennessy for me." She smiled her very best at the little man. "It has to do with his parentage—"

Right on cue, Missy cut her off, literally shoving the large box at her with a force that knocked her off balance.

"Tell Mr. Hennessy thank you. We'll just take these to the back room before we cause a traffic jam." Missy dazzled the men with her own best smile and grabbed quickly for the jeweler's box before Kelly could get breath to say more.

The two delivery men wasted no time taking the cue. The small one smiled. The tall one bowed and turned for the car.

"Mr. Hennessy asked me to have you call him later. He'll be in until eight," the other announced quickly before following out the door.

Kelly wasted no time in turning on Missy, her patience evaporating.

Missy grinned smugly, ignoring Kelly's threatening looks. "What would you do without me?" she asked as she handed the flowers to one of the other nurses and carried the other two boxes herself.

"You keep this up, and we'll all be forced to find out," Kelly warned, following the crowd.

They were picking up a few more people as they walked back toward the lounge. Kelly considered their glassy, voracious eyes with some trepidation and thought that the fun was dying fast. She was beginning to feel like the Pied Piper.

"It's no wonder he didn't have the guts to deliver these in person," she muttered to Missy who was still ignoring her. "He knows that I have any number of sharp instruments at my disposal."

She maintained a pained expression for all those envious faces, unwilling to admit that she was even more curious than they about just what was in those boxes.

Everyone filed into the twelve-by-twelve lounge until it looked like a staff meeting. Ellen, the nurse who'd grabbed the flowers, divided them among three plastic urinals filled with water, and set them out on a small table in the corner. Immediately the antiseptic atmosphere was transformed into springtime gardens. Everyone paused to take a deep breath before turning their attention to the mysteries at hand.

"Wish I had a sugar daddy like that to buy me presents."

"Matt Hennessy wouldn't have to buy me presents."

"Yeah, Kelly, when you see him, tell him what a cheap date I am."

"You're married. Give the single girls a chance."

Three days before, Kelly had talked about Matt Hennessy the same way, with the unabashed hunger of wishful humor. Since then, though, she'd met him. As she listened to the easy banter around her, Kelly was torn between telling them all that Matt Hennessy was just a nice guy who wasn't sure about all the fame that followed him around, and letting them know that he was a self-important jerk who thought he could always get his way because of who he was. The fact that he could be both of these and more didn't help her feel any more comfortable.

Missy hadn't waited for her. She was already elbow deep in tissue paper before Kelly even knew she'd opened the box.

"Oh, my God." Missy's eyes widened, and everyone leaned forward. Kelly leaned over for her own peek. She needn't have bothered. Missy took hold of the item, and slowly drew it from the box to the respectful murmurs of all present. In her hands, Missy held a beautiful black velvet formal, sleek, with simple lines that would surely mold carefully to a woman's figure. Sleeveless, its only ornamentation was a large, soft satin ruffle that traced the high neck, and plunged to a low V in the back. Kelly sat very still, realizing that her mouth was just as slack as everyone else's.

"Go try it on," Missy urged.

"No!"

"You're at dinner. Besides, the place is empty. What else do we have to do? I always knew that Matt Hennessy was good-looking and intelligent, but who'd guess he had such great taste? Simple but elegant, you know? And it's perfect for you, Kelly. If he'd gotten anything in taffeta or organza it would have taken us weeks to find you in all those ruffles."

"What's in the other box?" someone asked.

"Uh-uh," Missy shook her head. "We'll open it after Kelly's tried on the dress."

Kelly made a snatch for the other box, but Missy was still way ahead of her. With a smug grin, Missy handed over the dress.

It was a knockout, its lines fluid and elegant. The ruffle softly framed her throat and fell down her back to meet just this side of modesty. The material clung to her waist and swelled gently over her breasts and hips to suggest tantalizingly what lay beneath. Kelly could easily imagine herself wandering lazily around the decks of the *Delta Queen* on Matt's arm, bending to witty remarks, smiling secretly at their imagined relationship. She returned to the sound of applause.

"All right," Missy announced, "let's see what goes with it."

What went with it was a simple diamond-and-sapphire bracelet-and-earring set. The bracelet, which was a band of alternating stones, and the matching glittering hoops took Kelly's breath away.

"Oh, yea," Missy crowed, "another card." She held it carefully out of Kelly's reach. "'Kelly, darling. I thought these went better with the dress than the ones I bought you in August. Please me and wear them Friday.'" Pause. "Wow."

If Kelly didn't know any better she would have thought that Missy was beginning to believe the story herself.

"Where is everybody?"

Sister Agatha. Twelve people jerked upright like so

many startled rabbits and fled the lounge. Kelly turned just in time to see the tall nun fill the doorway, imperious impatience filling the stern eyes.

"And just what are you doing?" she demanded as if catching them behind the barn with cigarettes.

Kelly shrugged, the dress moving softly about her. "I'm taking my dinner break, Sister."

The nun took a slow look around the cluttered, fragrant lounge before letting her wintry gaze settle back on Kelly. "Not in that you're not. Get all of this mess out of here. And get out of that dress. It looks ridiculous."

The nun had already turned on her heel and departed by the time Kelly turned to Missy with a grin that reflected the madness of the afternoon. "And to think that I wore it just for her."

She didn't have to call Matt. He called her, no more than thirty minutes later. Just as Kelly put all of the gifts safely away until she could get off duty, she heard her name paged with undisguised excitement by a secretary who hadn't even gotten ruffled the day a private plane had hit the top floor of the hospital.

Kelly picked up the phone out at the triage desk where the crowd was more sparse. "Well, the entire hospital staff wants to be invited to the wedding," she said without preamble, "and security is checking the local police departments for reports of hot jewelry. Can you think of any other ways to make my life miserable?"

She heard him chuckle and was surprised by that same damn feeling of suffocation. "What's wrong? Didn't you like the dress?"

She intended to give no quarter. It was only fair after what he'd done. "Please tell me you rented it.

That way I can give it back instead of having to drop it down the incinerator chute."

"Of course not." He still thought it was funny. "Be careful of the baubles, though. They're Meredith's. Have you tried them on yet?"

"No," she lied, the picture of her in that dress still vivid. It had been so beautiful.

"You'll look great. That dress was made for you. I'll pick you up at six-thirty on Friday. We'll go out for drinks first. By the way, try to get off tomorrow, too. I got us tickets to the St. Louis Repertory."

Kelly almost groaned aloud. She would have given her right arm for those tickets. Tomorrow Meredith would be doing *Cat on a Hot Tin Roof,* and the reviews had been glowing.

"Matt, for once in your life, listen. I'm not going. I have any number of good reasons you wouldn't listen to anyway, so just listen to this. No."

"I didn't listen to that either. I told you, Kelly, you need some fun in your life."

"I'll buy a dog. Tell Meredith I'll get the jewelry back to her."

She was all set to slam the receiver back down on him, her mind made up, when out of nowhere Missy materialized and snatched it away from her.

"Matt Hennessy?" she asked glibly. "Hi, it's Missy Edwards; we met last night...nice to hear your sexy voice, too. Listen, don't worry about Kelly, she'll be there with bells on. She's just a little stubborn. What time tomorrow?...Okay, fine. Don't forget, her favorite wine is anything white, and her favorite restaurant is Eleven Eleven. You'll love it...oh, it's nothing. You can show your appreciation by making me your upstairs maid. Bye."

Turning on Kelly, she sighed dramatically, a hand

on her hip. "Sometimes I think you need a sitter. Why do you keep trying to turn that man down? Isn't he just about the most handsome thing you've seen on two legs?"

"That's not the point I'm trying to argue here."

"Don't you like the presents he gave you?"

"Missy, you're listening just about as well as usual..."

Again, Missy sighed. "Well, don't you?"

"They're beautiful. The jewelry is Meredith's."

"So what? Until two days ago, you wouldn't be allowed close enough to look at stuff like that, much less wear it. Give me one sane reason why you won't go out with him."

"Because..." Without warning her eyes filled with tears. "Because I'm finally learning to live without anticipation. I manage a day at a time and it's not too hard anymore."

She could feel herself deflating, her shoulders sinking as if under the weight of what she'd sought to accomplish in the time since Michael's death.

Missy took her by the shoulders. "Kelly, your life isn't over just because Michael's is. You've mourned him, and that's all you can be expected to do. Now it's time to go out and rejoin the world. Give Matt's idea a try. It can't hurt."

Kelly shook her head vehemently. "Why should I stroke his ego? He's only pushing so hard because he can't stand the idea of someone who won't fall in a dead faint at his feet."

At that, Missy's eyes widened noticeably and she actually gave Kelly a shake. "You're so dumb. Do you know what he said to me on the phone? He said, 'Black's for more than widow's weeds. Get her to find out before it's too late.' Kel, for all the fantasies who could have jumped into your car, you couldn't have gotten any better than Matt Hennessy. Keep that in mind when you make your decision."

Kelly spent the rest of the evening wrestling with the problem of Matt Hennessy and his offer. There was no question that she was intimidated by the idea. Even under normal circumstances she wasn't the kind of person to assume roles. She was Kelly Byrne, a twenty-eight-year-old nurse and widow, no more, no less. She had never had an urge to join the Thespians or the Junior League. She didn't know a Mercedes from a motorcycle, and couldn't find it in herself to get excited by a sale at Saks. Could someone like that carry off a stroll through the stratosphere of society without mortally embarrassing herself and her celebrated date?

On the other hand, her mother had told her never to impress anyone but herself. She'd never been intimidated by wealthy people before, and she'd had plenty of chances in all the years she'd worked around them. She was, in fact, just enough of a closet rebel to enjoy the fantasy of showing up rich people at their own game. She was afraid that she was going to have to admit that maybe it wasn't the show that bothered her so much. It might just be the leading man.

She still couldn't believe she'd reacted like that just to his touch. The thought of it made her pulse jump again. The idea of skyrockets and church bells had always seemed faintly ludicrous to her before. Marriage was friendship, comfort and respect. And yet Matt had set her off like a human torch.

As she instructed a woman on how to walk with crutches for her broken foot, Kelly remonstrated with herself over the idea that she should be stupid enough to court danger so flagrantly by even considering

Matt's offer. She wasn't really out of the woods yet, no matter what Missy or anybody might think. Michael's memory still tore at her unexpectedly, when she drove by the old restaurant or looked at the art posters they'd chosen together to decorate the bedroom walls. His loss was still a deep and tangible wound, and overcoming the terrible loneliness had become a daily struggle. So far, only a rigid attention to routine had brought her some small comfort. She couldn't possibly consider tampering with even that success. Especially with an emotional time bomb like Matt Hennessy.

While she started an IV on a child, she did her best to rail at the idea that Matt would think he could fashionably strong-arm her into a participating in his little game. Every time she considered how he failed to wait for her consent or increased the pressure by being so public with his approach, she couldn't help but remember how gentle his eyes were when he'd insisted she do it for her own sake.

As she sat down to complete her paperwork, she finally gathered the courage to identify the tightness in her chest. She was scared. Matt had blindsided her, appearing out of nowhere like a hot comet in her night sky. Within a matter of a few days, she had felt elation, exhilaration, trepidation and anticipation. She wanted to see him again, to accept his bribes and let him work his special magic on her to heal her loneliness. But she was just as afraid that when he left again, the light would go back out. She wasn't sure she could survive that.

By the time Missy helped her carry the booty out to the car, Kelly was thoroughly torn. It had been a long time since she'd known the dread of indecision. Butterflies had returned to her stomach like swallows home to the familiar shadows of Capistrano, and she found herself repeatedly wiping her sweaty palms against her jeans. The night was cool and crisp. A breeze tickled at the back of Kelly's neck, and a harvest moon cast a golden light in the sky. Kelly took a deep lungful of the autumn night to steady the uncertainty that was making her stomach burn.

"Well, you're going, aren't you?" Missy demanded as they negotiated bunches of flowers and boxes into the tiny space of Kelly's car. Kelly crawled in next to them and flipped the ignition switch, listening to the gentle rumble of the engine as it idled.

"I don't know," she admitted. "I guess we'll both know tomorrow night."

Later as she sped down the highway toward home, Kelly found herself still wrestling with the decision, and knew that she was in for a sleepless night. She wasn't looking forward to it at all.

CHAPTER 5

K elly didn't fall asleep until close to five, and by that time she still hadn't decided. It wasn't so much that she spent the time rehashing the debate she'd had with herself at work, or the contentions Missy and Matt had put forth. Instead she spent the time listening to the empty noises of her house.

The grandfather clock ticked gently from the entrance foyer, and down the hall a floorboard creaked. From the kitchen she could hear the low hum of the refrigerator as it kicked on. The heating system rattled a little in its old pipes, and beside her the white curtains rustled with the listless night wind that seeped in. Sounds of a house, but not of its people. The only human sounds that she could hear were her own.

She held her breath, listening. There were no snores, no sighs, no whispers that spoke of childhood secrets or adult dreams. There was no laughter in this house anymore. Kelly hadn't ever realized it before Matt had been there, but the house echoed like an empty well.

Kelly lay in the seemingly vast four-poster and stared at the shadows that lived among the corners of her room, now even more torn. Was Missy right? Had her own life become sterile in an attempt to avoid the pain of loss again? Had she drawn back so far that she might never find her way out into the open again? She couldn't deny the fact that her life had become rigid. It had become her protection when she thought she couldn't possibly have any defenses left. But perhaps her lifestyle had become too restrictive. Maybe she had died a little the night Michael had died.

It had been so long since she'd been so over-whelmed by the urge to giggle. But she'd wanted to giggle today. She couldn't ever remember finding her-self as plagued by as many conflicting emotions as the moment she'd walked out to find those two well-heeled men waiting for her attention. Even thinking about it now forced an unwanted grin to her lips. Matt had been high-handed about it, but he sure knew what strings to pull.

She wanted so much to escape the loneliness of that empty, echoing house. There had to be a way to bring the laughter back where it had once felt wel-come. Her life had become too quiet, too empty, like the rooms around her.

Kelly felt tears well up, tears born of frustration and the cold feel of an empty bed, and she let them fall. She just wished she weren't alone anymore.

～

WHEN SHE FIRST HEARD THE music, she thought that she was still dreaming, and it irritated her. She'd been flying over the Rockies, the wind ruffling through her hair and the sun setting too quickly to catch. Missy flew alongside drying her nail polish in the jet stream and offering suggestions on how to redecorate the landscape. With that kind of dream, she should have been hearing something Country-Western. What she was hearing was madrigal music.

She blinked, opening her eyes to the honey-colored light of morning. The window was still open to the crisp breeze. Outside she could hear the chatter of bird-song along the street and the distant hum of traffic.

And the music. Floating up from her lawn.

She lay very still for a moment, trying to make the quick jump to rationality. Like going to light speed in a flash; bang, you're awake. She had gotten good at it, since she had a lot of practice working at a place where she had to plug in her adrenaline on a moment's notice.

She did it now, sitting bolt upright, fully conscious and alert on only three hours sleep. And still she heard it.

From just beneath her window, a pleasant baritone voice crooned easily over the softly strummed chords of a lute. She stopped a moment longer, just to make sure. It really was a lute. The kind of instrument one expected to find in reenactments of medieval banquets, not the front lawn of a middle-class home in St. Louis. What on earth was going on?

Kelly jumped out of bed and ran to the window, not really taking the time to decide what she expected to find once she got there. What she saw immediately took the stuffings out of her knees. Thankfully, she had a wing-back chair set close to fall into, or she would have landed on the floor. She sat heavily and started out the window open-mouthed, fingers clenched to the sill as if it would help keep her world from turning over.

On her front lawn a snow-white horse draped in a

scalloped, sky-blue mantle that belonged in a jousting field munched lazily at her flowers. And it wasn't alone. Seated jauntily atop was the singer, decked out in glittering chain mail, leather boots and a blue cap with a feather that curled around to his back. He strummed at the lute and began another verse. It took Kelly a moment to find her own voice.

"For God's sake, Matt, what are you doing?"

He stopped and lowered the lute, a hand doffing his cap in a lofty sweep. "Ah, milady awakes!"

"Knock it off, Matt, this isn't Camelot! Just what do you think you're doing out there?"

He grinned up at her, the hat still held wide. "I thought it was pretty self-explanatory. I'm the white knight here to sweep you off your feet! Want another verse?"

"No!"

He paused a moment, considering. A car drove by, stopped, reversed and sat in the middle of the street watching.

"Don't you like it? Would you prefer something in art deco? I can come back in tie and tails with the Paul Whiteman Orchestra and do 'You're the Top.'"

"I'd prefer to go back to sleep! It's still the middle of the night!" She heard a screen door slam and knew that the neighbors were starting to respond again. A lady in the car had gotten out and now stood in the street to get a better view. And Matt wasn't about to budge. The Cheshire cat grin on his face told her that. She was plagued once more by that insane urge to giggle.

"Come on in and we'll talk about it," she tried.

He shook his head. "Not till you say that you'll go out with me."

It was hard to keep a straight face. "Matt, please! My yard isn't zoned for horses!"

"Either you say yes or I will!" the woman by the car called.

Kelly couldn't believe it. What had happened to her comfortably well-ordered life, her safe, quiet neighborhood where stability ranked three notches above school systems as a selling point? Kelly looked down at Matt seated nonchalantly on a horse who couldn't have been less interested, at the small crowd that was beginning to surreptitiously gather among the bushes along nearby lawns, at the lady who had traffic successfully blocked in order to watch the scene. And then she burst out laughing.

"Yes!" she yelled, struggling for breath, "now get in here!"

The crowd watched in amused silence. The lady got back into her car but still waited, unwilling to miss any more fun. Matt swung down from the horse and tied him neatly to the porch rail so he could go on eating Kelly's chrysanthemums.

Opening the door, Kelly ushered Matt inside. He'd ditched the chain mail for a blue sweatshirt, and with the boots on looked like a modern pirate. His grin was very self-satisfied, wrinkling the corners of his eyes.

"I knew you couldn't resist me," he told her as he walked through the door. "You just needed the right combination of romance and fantasy."

"Blackmail, you mean."

He shrugged easily and followed her to the kitchen. "Call it what you want. You'll change your mind about it after the next two weeks. Our reservations are for six tonight, by the way. Eleven Eleven." He sat down at the heavy oak table as Kelly walked over to put the coffee on. "Know what I like about you, Kelly? "

She didn't even turn around. "Besides my infinite patience? "

"Besides your infinite patience." She could hear the wry smile in his voice. "You don't go out of your way to impress anyone just because of his reputation."

She did turn around then to see that his wry attention was fixed on her clothes. She'd barely had time to get into a T-shirt and jeans before getting down to open the door. Her hair still tumbled haphazardly down her back. She grinned. "I don't care if the Pope had shown up on horseback. At this hour of the morning, I don't dress up for anybody." She handed over a cup of coffee and sat down. "Speaking of which, where did you find that get up?"

Grinning back, he tilted his chair against the wall and pointed at her chest. "You first."

Kelly looked down and had a grin herself. She'd thrown on a shirt that said in bright red: BOMB SQUAD: IF YOU SEE ME RUNNING, KEEP UP. "From a buddy. She traded me for a t-shirt that says 'ER Nurse: We can't fix stupid, but we can sedate it.' Now you."

He rested his coffee cup on his stomach. "Meredith. She got the Repertory people on it and voilà. I rode over from there. Do you know how hard it is to read a street map on horseback?"

Kelly had to laugh. She could just imagine what Missy would have to say when she heard about this. "Didn't anybody tell you that this isn't the back lot at MGM?"

"Anyplace can be the back lot at MGM. It just takes a little imagination." He accepted cream and a spoon and stirred at his coffee, the cup still balanced on his midriff. "I'm glad you said yes. I think the two of us will be the toast of the town."

Kelly had to admit that she was glad, too. No, relieved. Relieved that the decision had been made. She walked over and sat down opposite Matt, rubbing her chest a little at the alien feeling of exhilaration that had begun to settle there. It made her want to smile. It also scared her to death.

"My acceptance is conditional," she warned, struck by the idea even at that moment as she sipped at her coffee. Matt waited in comfortable silence for her stipulation. She faced him deliberately. "I know you've never been to this part of the Midwest before. Most people from the coasts think of it as the Beverly Hillbillies meet the Cleavers, and I'm tired of it. I'll go with you to your openings and things if you'll let me show you around the area. St. Louis is a beautiful place."

He never hesitated. "Condition accepted. I guess that means you won't introduce me to a hillbilly, though, huh?"

Kelly scowled over her cup. "You find one and I'll introduce you. Don't hold your breath, though."

He grinned. "Then I guess I'll have to settle for the grand tour. After seeing Webster, I have to admit that my curiosity's piqued. When were these homes built, turn of the century?"

Kelly nodded. "Mine was built in 1894. The rest of the old ones are from around then when Webster was a commuter stop on the train to the city. Like I said, real Americana."

"After coming off location in south Philadelphia, I think I could stand that," he said lightly, finishing the last of his coffee. Suddenly, he was checking his watch. "Okay, where do we start? We have until one o'clock. That's when I have to meet Meredith."

Kelly stopped, taken aback by his change of direction. "Now?"

"Why not?"

"Well, uh...I have housework, and, uh, Tuesday's my day to shop and pick up my cleaning, and—"

"Kelly," Matt remonstrated, righting his chair and leaning toward her. "Don't back out on me now. I'm accepting your offer. Teach me about St. Louis."

She looked around her as if for help. As usual, her house was spotless. Housecleaning was a safe ritual, and she performed it with religious regularity. Nothing really needed to be done that couldn't wait awhile.

"Do you have to get a permission slip from your parents?" he prodded.

"I don't have any—" she snapped without thinking. That was nothing he'd be interested in. More death, more nightmares. The same shadows of loneliness he offered to dispel. "I'm sorry. Your habit of dropping surprises in my lap before breakfast tends to make me a little testy. Of course we'll go. But someplace quiet. I'm still trying to wake up."

"I hope that doesn't mean churches," he said grinning mischievously. "I don't think either of us is quite dressed for it."

She grinned back. "The only thing you're dressed for is a joust. We'll compromise. The zoo, Shaw's Garden, maybe a stroll down by the arch."

"Sounds positively touristy."

"If you behave yourself, we could even go to the brewery."

"Brewery?"

Her eyebrows arched playfully. "Anheuser Busch."

His smile was positively delighted. "Now you're talking sight-seeing."

After Kelly changed into something a bit more appropriate, Matt rode the horse back to the Rep, and she followed in her car. The surreptitious looks she'd gotten in her neighborhood were nothing compared to the ones she got at the theater. By now, the story was all around, and everyone wanted to see the woman Matt Hennessy was wooing in medieval splendor. Matt not only failed to dispel their illusions, he went out of his way to encourage them, introducing Kelly around with warm smiles, possessively holding on to her hand as she walked, and helping her back into the car.

In point of fact, he spent the rest of the morning doing the same. The people at the zoo melted when he bought her balloons and hot dogs and held her hand as they strolled along the flower-lined walks. Heads turned as he bent close to listen to her and laugh, his eyes doting and happy.

Kelly had to admit that she was enjoying the performance almost as much as anyone else. Matt might have been playing a cameo today, but he still had the knack for sliding into character, and he was being the Matt Hennessy everyone seemed to want to see—the handsome, all-American movie star with just the right combination of charisma and humility. Just a boy with a million-dollar smile.

Every time he gazed down at her, or laughed happily into her eyes, Kelly envied herself. It was a scene straight from a movie. Crowds wandering aimlessly among the trees and man-made mountains, bright-colored balloons and train whistles, faint applause from the animal shows and the reflection of a cobalt sky in the seal basins where the inmates barked and children squealed. Real Audrey Hepburn stuff, and Kelly was Audrey. She felt like one of those bright silver balloons that had to be tied tightly to keep from floating away.

The crowds were more sparse at Shaw's Garden, the locals' name for the Missouri Botanical Garden, which was just as well. Kelly didn't want to hurry through the carefully manicured lawns and still-brilliant flower beds. The Garden was for meditating, and that was hard to do with a hundred greedy eyes and ears following you. She and Matt strolled through the lush humidity of the Climatron, where a tropical jungle lay trapped within the first geodesic dome ever built, and sat in the cool stillness of the wildflower garden. It took them almost an hour to get through the rose gardens where the last of the tenacious flowers still filled the air with their sensuous aroma. They wandered along the rambling paths, holding hands like kids.

For the grand finale, Kelly took Matt to the immense Japanese garden. Laid out with an Oriental precision and simplicity that always amazed Kelly, the garden spread out from any point of observation in perfect harmony and understated grace. Waterfalls tumbled over precisely arranged boulders. Gumdrop islands dotted great lagoons spanned by delicate arched bridges. Every tree, flower, rock had been meticulously designed to present a pleasing and serene atmosphere. The framed pictures she and Michael had taken here decorated her family room.

She and Matt made it no further that day. They sat at one end of the gardens for close to two hours and enjoyed the peace.

"Kelly," he said finally, out to the clouds, his arm easily over her shoulders, "there's something I think you should know."

Kelly didn't bother to look over from where she considered the view. "What's that?"

He motioned with his other hand. "This isn't the brewery."

Kelly couldn't help but grin. "Damn, Matt, you're alert."

"I realized it when I didn't smell any hops. You promised to take me to the brewery."

She turned her head to see the noon sun warm the planes of his face. "You don't like it here?"

"Sure. I just..."

"You should see it in the spring," she said, turning back to the view.

She knew Matt was grinning. "The brewery?"

"The garden. I decided to save the brewery for a day when the weather's bad. Today was too good to miss this."

"You mean the weather isn't always perfect here?" he demanded playfully.

She shook her head, her eyes on the garden. "That's only in California. In the Midwest, we pride ourselves on our contrasts."

Kelly examined an area at their feet, a rock garden that had been raked into fluid design around carefully arranged shrubs and boulders that cleanly framed the angular water reeds beyond, the vast reflection of water and sky, the bridges, the tea house. And the trees, variegated into fire by the autumn. Kelly sighed, the serenity of the place and Matt's company seeping in like sunlight.

Matt lifted his head to let the sun wash his face and then returned his gaze to the water. "I think I would like to come back in the spring and see this."

"Oh, I don't know," Kelly teased. "After all, St.

Louis is so provincial. The weather might not be perfect."

He paused a moment as if in consideration. "Yeah, you're right. Never mind."

Kelly smacked him playfully in the ribs.

MISSY WAS WAITING on the porch when Kelly pulled up. Slowly rocking back and forth in one of Kelly's wicker rockers, she stopped working on her nails long enough to wave a greeting as Kelly reached the steps.

"Do you want to hear the news now, or would you rather wait till the phone rings? I've spent the morning steeping myself in recent folklore, you know. I don't know if you realize it, but this neighborhood is all atwitter, and I wouldn't be at all surprised if the mini-cam showed up any minute now." She leaned back, gesturing elegantly with a hand. "'Local girl says yes to knight in shining armor.' I don't suppose you took pictures for your adoring public."

Kelly walked by without a word so that Missy was forced to gather her nail paraphernalia together and follow her in.

"So, you're going?" she persisted, undaunted. "My stellar logic convinced you, huh? I knew it would. You never could resist reason. Or tall, dark men with green eyes, it seems. Why didn't you bring him back home to see me? Ashamed of your friends? I think you just don't want the competition."

"He's with Meredith."

Missy grimaced. "Yeah, well. So, his taste runs more to blonde and frigid. I think he's a fool, myself. He picks someone who's brilliant, talented, famous and beautiful, when if he really tried, he could have had you. Or better yet, me."

Kelly offered a dry grin from the sink where she rinsed out the coffee cups. "Thanks, I think the next two weeks is about all I can handle."

Missy leaned against the cabinet and blew at her nails. "I think that if you really worked on it, you could get the inside track. I mean, what's Meredith Mason got that you don't? Matt Hennessy shouldn't waste his time with actresses. They're unstable. What he needs is a nice, normal Midwest girl who'll keep his feet on the ground."

"Missy," Kelly snapped a bit more hotly than she'd intended. "It's a game, remember?"

Missy arched an eyebrow at her. "Don't yell at me. I'm on your side. I'm just here to make you look good for your big debut, and then I fade back into the shadows."

"But if it's all the same with me, you'll be here when Matt shows up later."

"Of course." Missy's smile was the soul of equanimity. "Somebody has to chaperone."

MATT SEEMED delighted to see Missy again, dropping a kiss on her forehead without being asked. For her part, Missy kept herself from babbling or drooling, and stated unabashedly that she was quite proud of herself for it, considering how good Matt looked in a three-piece suit.

Kelly couldn't have agreed more. Some tailor had drawn the dark blue pinstripe suit over the long lines of Matt's frame like a glove, the crisp cream shirt complementing it perfectly. It even looked as if the tie was invented just to look good on Matt. Kelly felt almost shabby in comparison.

It was still warm enough for her to make use of her good cream linen suit, and she wore it with a sapphire blouse. Her hair fell straight and full over her shoulders without ornamentation. Too simple, she thought uncomfortably. She'd look out of place next to him.

But when he assessed her, his eyes lit with a frank appreciation that warmed her. She found herself smiling, a little embarrassed, and wished fervently that she could brassily laugh the whole thing off like Missy.

"Don't you know it's bad form to upstage the star?" Matt demanded with a mischievous grin, and she was pleased.

Even for the fact that they weren't left alone for a minute, they had a lovely evening. A chauffeured limousine carried them to Richard Perry where they dined on veal Oscar and a triple chocolate cake that left Kelly speechless, then they went on to the theater. Reporters and fans followed everywhere, harassing Matt with questions. Kelly just stood by quietly and smiled, taking her cues from him.

As she saw him become his public self, she realized that this was a completely different person than the one she'd gotten to know. He smiled and nodded, speaking in a perfectly even, well-modulated voice. His eyes gave the impression of total attention. He made everyone who approached him feel as if they knew him well. And yet Kelly could see, even in the slightly stooped posture he assumed when he wanted to appear relaxed and easy-going, that he was completely in control, alert and on guard. He was at work.

As Kelly recognized that, she realized Matt had never been that person with her. They had always been like two people who'd just met in a coffee shop, always talking about his family or her work and the cities where they grew up. They had never even acknowledged his idol status except in jest when dealing directly with fans. That made Kelly feel unaccountably special and fueled the giddy excitement of the evening even more. That silver balloon was straining to be free.

Inevitably, as reporters pursued, Matt brought Kelly over to be introduced, his arm protectively around her waist, his eyes smiling the possessively happy smile he'd worn all day. And following his lead, she answered the press's questions with what she called her Princess Diana smile.

Yes, she had been seeing Matt, but they'd enjoyed their privacy too much to want the story leaked any sooner than necessary. Yes, soft laugh and familiar glance at Matt, he had shown up on her lawn on a charger that morning, but she hadn't said yes to the question everyone presumed. He'd just decided that now the story was out, he wanted to introduce her to the press properly. She, being somewhat shy by nature, had hesitated, so he'd used his own unique style of persuasion. And wasn't it all worth it, Matt concluded with a hug and a kiss to the top of her head. After all, Kelly was something to show off. Pictures were taken, curiosity salved, and they made their third-row seats before the lights went out.

"I know talent when I see it," he said quietly in her ear while everyone thought him to be professing his undying love. "You do that very well. Want a screen test?"

Shifting in his seat, he slipped an arm around Kelly's shoulders. She started, realizing without the distraction of lights and reporters' questions, that her reaction to Matt's touch didn't necessarily ease with familiarity. His fingers massaged her shoulders as he talked, tracing lazy circles over her tingling skin. Kelly did her very best to stay still and concentrate on something else, anything else. Pulling away from him at this point would provoke unwanted speculation.

It didn't work too well. Kelly couldn't decide whether she couldn't move or couldn't sit still. Trying not to think how pleasant it felt, she leaned her head back and smiled up at him with what she thought would be loving eyes.

"Try not to spread it so thick next time," she cooed under her breath. "At one point, I wasn't sure whether you considered me your date or your Labrador retriever."

He chuckled, his eyes lazily taking in hers. Kelly didn't move. She was beginning to feel oddly smothered, as if something were crowding her air. She shouldn't have moved. Matt was too close; she couldn't scoot over to get room. She felt a trembling set in. Felt the press of people around her, watching. She had no business being in this theater. It was too hot. Too crowded, and she suddenly decided that she didn't want to sit still. She wanted to get away to the cool emptiness of her home.

Matt leaned over her upturned face and took her chin in his hand. His touch so very gentle, he drew a finger along the taut line of her jaw. Kelly never saw the flash as he bent to her. She caught her breath, suffocating. She could feel his breath against her cheek, her ear. Holding her still, he kissed her, his lips as soft as his cheek. Clean-shaven and smooth, smelling of forests and night.

She knew that her eyes had closed. She didn't realize that her hand had come up, that it had instinctively found the line of his throat where the pulse bounded against her fingers. She couldn't move from him, from the searching of his lips and the brief taste of his tongue. It was all she could do to keep from sighing or weeping.

He pulled away, his face still close above hers, the house lights illuminating an intensity in his eyes that drew Kelly to him, her heart pounding. He looked as if he'd just discovered something, and that it troubled him. He seemed to be a little out of breath, too. Then, with what Kelly recognized as a deliberate move of separation, Matt smiled.

"The fans should be pleased. Thanks."

Kelly's answering smile was even more tenuous than Matt's. "Anytime, Paul."

Moments later, the theater fell into darkness. Kelly was relieved, needing the darkness to right her senses before facing the public again.

She was going to have to be far more careful if she wanted to come out of these two weeks intact. Matt could be dangerous for her. Even now, halfway through the first scene, she had trouble hearing the dialogue for the rushing of blood in her ears. That was definitely something that had never happened to her before. It was intoxicating, and she found herself wanting more. Wanting to feel that strange electricity his fingers generated against her skin, and bask beneath the gentle delight in his eyes. It had been too long since a man had looked at her like that, and she realized how very much she'd missed it.

And yet, she knew that it was only a transient thing. In two weeks, Matt would leave and she would have to try and weave this moment of magic into a life that until just a few days ago seemed to have been enough. She would have to survive these beautiful days with Matt just as she had her days alone. And if she were very lucky and very careful, and if Matt didn't repeat this evening's performance more than a very few times, she'd probably make it.

The first act ended, and Matt turned to her with the smile that had set the crowd on its ear. And Kelly began to think as she smiled back, her heart leaping in her chest with the pleasure of it, that it might end up being a very long two weeks after all.

CHAPTER 6

"I haven't seen a shot like that since *Gone With the Wind*."

Kelly looked up from the bland cafeteria lunch she'd been considering without relish to see the unholy enthusiasm in Missy's eyes as she gazed down at the newspaper. Missy had worked miracles to pull the two of them to days for the two-week duration, and had managed to be on hand for Matt's arrival each night. She'd considered it her duty, she'd said, deftly arranging Kelly's life around the nightly trips to Wonderland without the slightest hint of jealousy or resentment. She seemed to take a genuine delight in playing the part of fairy godmother, and Kelly was glad. Missy had done more during this crazy time to help her than anyone else.

"What is?" asked Valerie Jackson, one of the other nurses, leaning over for a peek. Missy just pointed.

Valerie looked, raised her head at Kelly and gaped. "Oh, my God."

Immediately other heads craned for looks, and Kelly found more astonished eyes on her.

"All right, what's up?"

Missy grinned, turning the paper to her. The picture that had caught everyone's eye had been taken the night of the theater. Someone had snapped the shot just as Matt had leaned to kiss her, his fingers on her chin. There was no mistaking the look in her eye, and it made her catch her breath. Without another word, she got to her feet and stalked off.

Missy followed. "Good move. You're not used to your privacy being so blatantly invaded. Matt's right. You're good at this sort of thing. Ever think of asking him to arrange a screen test?"

Kelly swung on her heel, intent on saying something. One look at the sly amusement in Missy's eyes made her realize that she had nothing to say. She turned again without a word and kept on walking.

So did Missy. "Let Meredith Mason eat cake."

Kelly made it back to the ER and escaped out to her post at the triage desk to hide from the majority of inquisitive staff for a while. The triage nurse acted as a kind of air traffic controller, assessing the patients when they first arrived and directing the course of their care according to the type and severity of complaint. Today it seemed that not many people needed her help, so Kelly was left pretty much alone with her thoughts. And her thoughts kept going back to that picture.

She had the definite feeling that things were beginning to get way out of hand, and she knew why. She was not only doing just what Missy had predicted, she was afraid she was doing just what she'd predicted. She was having a good time.

The limelight hadn't bothered her as much as she'd thought. She had been able to visit the lovelier restaurants of the city and then stroll with Matt along the neighborhood parks with just as much ease as she had before. The frequent press of fans and reporters was no more than a constant source of private amusement between them. Maître d's hustled and politicians surreptitiously stared. From a life in the mainstream of Middle America, Kelly suddenly found herself tasting all of the rarefied treats her city had to offer. And damn it, she was enjoying it. She had also begun to anticipate seeing Matt. And that was the problem.

She'd never known anyone like him. As time passed and they'd become more comfortable with each other, he'd begun to let her in on just what lay beneath the gloss and brash confidence. He was exciting and intelligent, his mind like lightning that could strike a dozen different directions at once. His sense of humor was often directed at his own expense, and he had an unconscious knack for making Kelly feel unique. She discovered that he had more fun in the noisy, overcrowded Italian family restaurants of The Hill neighborhood than at the more expensive, formal ones. He loved horses and listened to music with his eyes closed. One minute Kelly could be disturbed and unsettled by his touch, the next she could feel as if he were her oldest friend.

She found herself ignoring the certainty of his departure. Worse, she'd begun to catch the first flashes of resentment in reaction to his mention of Meredith.

If only Meredith Mason were stupid or ugly or bitchy, it might have been different. Kelly could feel self-righteously indignant, telling herself that Matt was a fool being attracted to her. But Meredith was none of these. Matt had chosen a class act.

After their night at the theater, Meredith had greeted them at the dressing room door with a smile that glowed. Kelly couldn't take her eyes off the porcelain skin, deep brown eyes and the legendary Mason hair. Perfect, almost white-blonde—real, from what the gossips said.

"I recognize you," the beautiful actress greeted her, hand on slim hip. "Your picture's in all the papers. Isn't it fun?" The question was asked tongue-in-cheek, and Kelly couldn't help but grin as she followed Matt in.

Meredith shut the door behind them so that they were alone. Kelly immediately gave in to the urge to look around. She'd never been in a dressing room. There was the obligatory mirror ringed in bare lights and a rack against the far wall with costumes. But the vanity where Kelly would have expected a jumbled mess of telegrams, makeup and personal mementos, was arranged in almost sterile order. And only one bouquet of flowers decorated the otherwise bare room. Roses. Three dozen of them. It embarrassed Kelly that they should make her angry.

"Please sit down," Meredith spoke up, her naturally rich voice a little husky. "Kelly, I hope Matt's told you what a good sport you are. I have a feeling that once he made up his mind about this, he didn't give you much of a chance to say no." The look she gave Matt was almost maternal.

Kelly laughed, now at ease with the woman. "I'd say she has a pretty good handle on you, Matt."

He grimaced. "Should I leave you two alone so you can talk behind my back?"

"Not on my account," Kelly grinned. "I'm perfectly happy seeing you squirm for a change."

Meredith's laughter was surprised and delighted.

The three of them left an hour later and stopped at a coffee house before dropping Kelly off. The conversation was congenial, and Kelly enjoyed it. It was only later as she lay in bed that she realized that while Meredith was one of the foremost experts on theater, she had little time left for anything else. They'd talked about theater, movies, agents and mutual friends in the business. And at that point, Kelly had realized what Meredith and Matt talked about when they were alone. She'd thought it a bit stifling. But you couldn't hate a person for singleness of mind.

But now it was three o'clock and time to head home. Kelly had a lot of getting ready to do tonight. She'd just finished giving a report to the incoming nurse when she saw someone waiting for her just beyond the desk. Oh Lord, she thought, she'd completely forgotten him. The anxious look on his face made her angry with her neglect.

"Rich, hi," she said, walking over. "I'm sorry I haven't talked to you. Things have been a little hectic lately."

A brief, wry grin flashed into his eyes. "I know. I've been reading about it. I'm, uh...happy for you."

"Happy..." For a moment she forgot. He didn't know. She'd meant to explain, but had never had the chance. "Oh, Rich, no. No, you don't understand. I'm not really dating Matt. I'm helping him out."

Rich was beginning to look confused. Kelly held up a hand and took a moment to think before taking him aside to explain what the situation really was. By the time she finished, Rich looked a little less confused and a lot less unhappy.

"I just couldn't understand why you hadn't said something, you know?" he admitted uncomfortably. He looked briefly at his shoes, his ears pinking a little.

"I'm sorry," she said, placing a hand on his arm. "It's been such a circus the past few days that I'm having trouble just keeping my head above water."

He smiled. "Fun, huh?"

At first, Kelly grimaced. Then she shrugged and

nodded, her grin a little guilty in the face of Rich's gentle candor. "Yeah, I guess it really is. It'll be just as nice to get back to bike riding and movies, though. I don't think I'm meant for this life."

He nodded. "Well, let me know. And, uh, tell Matt hi for me."

"I will," she said with a grin.

She did like Rich. He was like a calm pool—quiet, peaceful, caring. Kelly was grateful that he was her friend.

By the time Matt was due to arrive, Kelly had already been dressed for half an hour. Missy, working herself into a fever of anticipation, had personally overseen every area of Kelly's preparation. She'd done Kelly's nails and makeup, bringing out the almost startling blue in Kelly's eyes to the point that the too-cute pug nose and small mouth could almost be overlooked. She arranged Kelly's hair into a loose knot that spilled curled tendrils around her neck. Designed, Missy had assured her, to be pulled down by loosening one pin. Missy had even chosen the appropriate perfume and stockings for the "best effect."

At one point, when Missy had laid out the proper bath powder and deodorant, Kelly had dryly informed her that Samurai didn't go through this much ritual to meet their deaths. Missy had dismissed the comment with a wave of her hand and an airy retort that since Kelly was fulfilling Missy's favorite fantasy, Missy had every right to make sure Kelly didn't spoil it. Kelly gracefully acquiesced.

By the time Kelly was ready to everyone's satisfaction, Missy was close to driving her nuts. She decided to escape into the kitchen on the premise of rectifying a dry throat. It was an honest enough excuse. Kelly stood alone in the empty kitchen and wiped distractedly at the clean countertop as she waited for the doorbell to ring.

When it did, she turned abruptly toward it. Her reflection flashed at her from the night-darkened window, and she was forced to stop, still startled by the alien feel of it. She looked like another person, someone she didn't know. Her eyes sparkled with the skill of Missy's art, her features highlighted expertly. Her hair framed her face delicately and gave her the dignity of additional height. Diamonds and sapphires glittered against the mass of ebony hair. Kelly couldn't resist turning her head to catch the light in them. Circling her arm perfectly, the bracelet accentuated the slender line of her arms. The dress fit her like a fantasy, its liquid grace breathtaking. The picture was one of sophistication, and Kelly couldn't help but feel a bit overwhelmed.

The sight of Matt in a black tuxedo made it worse. He was every woman's fantasy, filling the clothes as if they'd been created just for him. Kelly realized after a moment that she'd forgotten to breathe.

Missy stood between them, her head rotating back and forth like a spectator at a tennis match, satisfaction smeared all over her face. After a moment of silence all around, she finally lost her patience.

"Well, aren't you going to tell me what a good job I did? I feel like the original Fairy Godmother, you know. And to think that just yesterday she was no more than a pumpkin. Now she's going to the ball with Prince Charming."

"You're babbling," Kelly said, grinning dryly, somewhat regaining her own composure.

Missy shrugged agreeably. "Overwhelming beauty does that to me."

Kelly grinned at Matt, concurring. "She's not talking about me, you know."

"She should be," Matt marveled with a slow shake of the head. "I can't believe how different you look."

Kelly scowled at the left-handed compliment. "And to think," she said over to Missy, "I didn't even have to shave my beard to do it."

Matt moved now, walking up and making a motion for Kelly to turn. She obliged, arms out for inspection.

"No," he said with a firmer shake of his head. "I didn't mean that you look more beautiful than you did. Just...different. You're like a chameleon. I think I'm having trouble keeping up with you."

Kelly almost let out another retort, her usual defense when threatened with being overwhelmed. The evening hadn't even started yet, and she was already feeling as if she couldn't breathe properly. She was caught tight between the image she'd trapped in the window and the frank delight in Matt's eyes. His words were sincerely complimentary, the pleasure at seeing her dressed up reflected in his eyes. She didn't want to do anything that would steal away that happy smile.

"In that case," she said quietly to him, "thank you."

With unconscious grace, Matt took her face in his hands and smiled down at her, his eyes calling up all the moments they'd spent together. "You keep surprising me like this, and I'm not going to give you back after two weeks. The way you look tonight, I'm going to have to be on my toes to keep you from being stolen away from under my nose."

Just the bright warmth of those green eyes was enough to ignite a sore sweetness in her chest. His touch was robbing her knees of strength.

"Probably be just what you deserve," she said,

grinning even more hesitantly, her eyes wide. "It'd make you more careful about inviting strange women to premieres."

He didn't move to take his hands away but an amused smile touched his lips. "I wish you could see yourself right now. You look like somebody just pushed you to the edge of the cliff. Enjoy the view, Kelly."

Kelly pulled away, his touch suddenly too intimate. She realized with an unpleasant start that she'd actually forgotten Missy was in the room.

She made it a point to smile dryly. "Lighten up a little, Matt, or I won't go at all."

His grin broadened conspiratorially. "Sure you will. I'm not going to miss watching you put all those rich socialites to shame."

"If we're doing *My Fair Lady* now," she said, smiling sweetly, "the accent's all wrong."

She reached for her black cape, but Matt took it from her hands, swirling it with a flourish to her shoulders. "Just remember that those longing glances I give you tonight won't be all acting," he said, smiling.

"Good thing, too." Missy spoke up from behind Kelly, making her want to jump. "I'd hate to think I wasted my afternoon over here."

Matt turned to grin at the tall blonde and then back to Kelly. "When the live mini-cam shows up, please tell them that Matt Hennessy is taking great delight in his new lady love. She's as bright as she is beautiful."

"My pleasure," Missy assured him, hurrying to open the door like a mother sending off her prom-bound daughter. Kelly gathered her purse and turned to take Matt's proffered arm, reading in his eyes a pleasure that sent a shiver flushing through her like a shower of hot sparks.

"Oh my God!" Missy cried, distracting her.

Kelly looked over to see her friend peering through the door and out into the fading light of dusk.

"Oh, my God," Missy echoed more breathlessly, "I have to get a picture of this. Nobody's going to believe it! Matt, you've outdone yourself! I just can't believe it."

Kelly reached the door just then and took her own look. She, too, stood staring into the night, her mouth a little slack.

Outside on the pavement of her quiet Webster street, surrounded by shyly excited children and one or two adventurous adults, stood a hansom cab. Imitation gaslights glowed warmly at the sides, and high on the driver's seat a green-liveried driver held the reins to a set of exquisite matched bays.

Kelly and Missy turned as one to Matt's self-satisfied grin for explanation.

He shrugged amicably. "Even though I've never been to St. Louis, I still have a few connections here. A grateful ex-client was more than happy to help."

Kelly knew what he was talking about. Matt's first picture had been financed outside of Hollywood, a small-budget epic that no one expected would make it. One of the lucky financiers who had made a seven-hundred-percent profit on his investment happened to live in the area.

"Besides," Matt said, squeezing Kelly's arm, "I couldn't let my image as a romantic hero slide. This seemed the only appropriate transportation for Cinderella."

"Be careful," Kelly warned lightly, "in five minutes you've elevated yourself from language professor to prince."

The crowd was swelling outside. The horses stood patiently as people tentatively reached to stroke their necks, and the footman waited in polite silence through the first hesitant questions. Then with a screech the mini-cam truck slammed to a halt two houses down.

"Well, at least I didn't have to call them," Missy said with a grin. "I think your public awaits, kids. Kelly, stand up straight and smile so I know we're enjoying ourselves. Matt, you look just fine the way you are."

"Thank you, Missy. We'll tell you all about it when we get back."

"No you won't," she said, grinning mischievously. "I'd just be in the way."

Kelly turned to let off a nasty retort, but Matt deftly propelled her out the door and into the lights of the waiting public.

"I get time-and-a-half for this."

He kept smiling toward the camera. "What for?"

"Having to talk to this reporter. He tried to have me fired last month for not taking care of him quickly enough."

Matt did look over then, ironic surprise in his eyes just as the reporter in question zeroed in on them.

"Are you surprised, Miss Byrne?" the man asked a moment later.

Kelly let an eyebrow arch at the smarmy look on the man's face. "Astounded," she said, wishing she could tell his viewing audience why. She could see that look of warning on Matt's face, though, and managed a too-sweet smile. "Of course, I should know better by now. Matt is always thinking of romantic things like this."

"Like what else?"

"Well—" she smiled, beaming up at Matt and using the natural talent he'd claimed for her, "—he gave me these earrings in a box of Cracker Jacks. Imagine. I bit into one and almost lost a filling."

Before anyone could think to stop her, she turned to the camera and showed the man the filling in question. The cameraman was grinning from ear to ear. The reporter looked as if he'd just stepped in something. Matt, his reactions admirably quick, offered a few quick platitudes in closing and propelled her along to where the coachman waited to help her into the carriage.

That was almost a mistake. The carriage was so high up that the first step was above her knees. But once again, Matt, with fore-planned grace, outdid his image. Sweeping her into his arms, he carried her into the coach himself.

"Can't I even say good-bye?" she asked in all innocence with an adoring smile the camera couldn't miss.

They saw Matt smile sweetly back. "One more word out of you, and I'll probably end up dropping you on your head."

Kelly shook her head resignedly. "They just don't make princes as charming as they used to."

CHAPTER 7

M att climbed into the rich brown leather seat and turned to tap on the roof. Kelly could hear the coachman settle in on top and the first clatter of reins as the horses took off. Two small electric lamps lit the interior of the cab with a soft yellow glow that could easily be taken for the original gaslight. Rich cream curtains framed the windows. Across from where she and Matt were seated the solid brown leather interior broke into compartments for storage, and a deep-pile coffee-colored carpet cradled Kelly's feet. Even for the noise of the horses' hooves against concrete and asphalt, Kelly couldn't imagine a smoother, more comfortable ride. It was as if they floated through the streets, the darkening panorama passing silently by the windows.

As much as she might have tried, she couldn't help but be swept up in the fantasy Matt had created for her. She might as well have been traveling through the streets of nineteenth-century London on the way to Covent Garden. She certainly wasn't in St. Louis.

As she watched, Matt reached into two separate compartments to produce a bottle of chilled *Pouilly-*

Fuissé and glasses, and then a small package of warm canapés he set out on a small foldout table that had been ingeniously camouflaged into the leather. He handed her a glass and raised his own in a toast.

"To fantasies," he said, smiling over at her, his eyes soft and beguiling.

Kelly raised her own glass, unable to keep from returning his smile. "All right; this time you have me. I'll toast to that."

She sipped her wine, the fine full liquid deliriously warming the icy anxiety that curled in the pit of her stomach.

"This is better than the time we decorated one of the operating rooms like a school gym and had a dance."

Matt saw the mischief in Kelly's eyes and grinned back. "Formal attire?"

She nodded. "Black tie and scrub suits. I was escorted to the dance in an ambulance."

"An ambulance, huh?" he countered, sipping at his wine. "That might have been better than this. Sirens and flashing lights."

"Nah," Kelly disagreed with a definite shake of her head. "Might be romantic for you, but the sound of a siren just gives me the urge to grab a stethoscope. I'm much more partial to the horses."

He nodded agreeably. "I'll remember that."

Kelly looked up at the twinkle in his eyes. "You do have a habit of doing things like this, don't you?"

"Of course—" he smiled delightedly "—I have a tradition to uphold."

"Whose? Douglas Fairbanks, Jr., or Cary Grant?"

"My father. He's been pulling this kind of thing on my mother for over thirty-five years. He did the white knight routine when they were in their forties."

"And I thought it was an original," she objected playfully.

Matt refilled her glass before she had a chance to refuse. She hadn't had much to eat all day, and the wine was going straight to her head. At least it was warming her up.

"I can't think of much my parents haven't done," he said. "You know that line you gave the reporter about the Cracker Jacks? That was how my mother got her engagement ring. I thought you'd found out about it somehow."

Kelly laughed, the image a delightful one. "How do you get away with pulling that stuff on Meredith? She doesn't strike me as the type for it."

"She's not. She tends to call it superfluous and silly."

Kelly thought of that almost stark dressing room and nodded. "Danish furniture."

"What?"

She turned to see Matt's confusion and chuckled. "I've been hanging around Missy too long. She would have understood immediately. What I meant was that Meredith is a person made up of clean lines. No frills. Like Danish furniture."

"Oh." He popped a canapé in his mouth and swallowed it in one motion. "I'd never thought about it that way, but you're right. Sometimes, though, I think she's missing out on too much. There's a lot to be said for a little craziness in your life."

Kelly nodded absently as she followed Matt's example, her tone dry. "It sure has done wonders for mine. I can't even go to the bathroom without eight people offering to help just in case I'm planning a secret rendezvous in there with you."

"That's because of who I am, not how I carry on my love affairs."

"Don't bet on it. If I get one more request for the story about the white knight, I'm going to just give it to the *Enquirer* and be done with it."

He nodded with suspiciously grave eyes. "It's just too bad it's not any fun."

Kelly shook her head as she took a sip. "That's the problem. It's too much fun."

Her answer provoked a wide delighted smile. "I was hoping you'd finally admit it. For a while there, I was afraid nothing was going to bring you back to life."

Kelly turned to him, her eyebrows arched as she took another sip. "I really wish you wouldn't insist on talking about me as if I were a prisoner."

"Maybe that's how you strike me," he said, pulling the bottle back out to top off the almost-full glasses.

She shook her head. "I'm just a working girl who likes the quiet things in life."

"No," he said, "you haven't been. Do you know what I saw in you tonight that was so special?"

"Three hours of Missy's primping and an excellent wardrobe," she scoffed.

He refused to treat the subject with humor. Replacing the bottle, he turned his attention back to her, taking hold of her free hand. Kelly looked down and was oddly struck by the sinewy grace of his long fingers. He had musician's hands within which he should collect the fruits of his imagination and soul. He grasped her hand as if his own life force could endow it with his own strength and will. Kelly felt inexplicably moved, as if she were seeing an act of great compassion.

When he lifted his eyes to her, they pierced her

with the honesty of their concern. "Tonight for the first time since I've known you," he said quietly, "I saw anticipation. Until now, I've dragged you along by brute force, and you've grudgingly had a good time. Tonight whether you know it or not, you broke free and admitted to yourself that you could enjoy life again—that there's more than just working to numb the pain."

Unable to bear the sudden sincerity in his gentle eyes, Kelly turned to look out the window. In the mauve and coral dusk, house lights flickered through shuddering trees. Cars passed and slowed, some honking happily at the coach that shared their road.

"There's something I don't understand, Matt," she finally said, her voice small with the effort of asking. "Why did you bother? It wasn't just Meredith, or you could have asked any one of a thousand girls to help. Missy was ready to sell chances."

He gently squeezed her hand. "Because you're special. You make me remember that Matt Hennessy's more than what's revealed in *Newsweek*. And that he's not all he's cracked up to be. Kelly, you're worth more than a hundred people I deal with every day, and you deserve more than you let yourself have." His smile grew warmer, more open. "I get lost sometimes in the myth of Matt Hennessy. In just a week with you, I've found myself right back where I belong. And it makes me feel better than I have in years."

Kelly was assailed by that bright balloon again, so full and warm it should burst in her. She could only face the growing attraction in those warm, soft eyes for a moment, their fervor threatening to suffocate her. He frightened her when he said things like that, not because she didn't want to hear them but because she did. Those were just the words she wanted Matt to say to her.

As she struggled for some kind of objectivity, she realized that she didn't feel that way because he was Matt Hennessy the film star. When he was with her that person was no more than a game. She felt that way because when Matt was with her he was a madman with the gentlest eyes she'd ever seen.

"And in the past week," she answered quietly, her eyes on the rich black velvet that fell over her knees, "you've managed to get me back into forward gear."

He took her hand again. "Scary?"

She took a long, calming breath, sure he could hear her heart. "Terrifying. I've been on hold for almost two years."

For a moment Matt held her face up, his fingers beneath her chin. "Like I said before, Kelly. Enjoy the view. You're ready for it."

Kelly wasn't sure she was even breathing. Matt's eyes were locked into hers with an intensity that filled her like hot wine. She saw the attraction, the tenderness and a kind of surprise, as if he were discovering something new in either her or himself. She knew for sure that she didn't want to move, couldn't even if she'd tried. Bound to Matt by the featherweight touch of his fingers and the communion of his eyes, she didn't know if she was more happy or frightened by the growing candor in his gaze. There was more there than she'd ever asked for...more than she thought she could handle. And not as much as she wanted.

Kelly hadn't felt the carriage come to a stop, but even as Matt finally let go his hold of her, the door next to him opened. She saw the coachman stand aside to help them out.

Matt brought Kelly's hands to his lips. "Time to go

share you with everybody else." His voice carried genuine regret. His eyes in the pale yellow light told Kelly
that they were about to play a scene for an audience.
They also told her that the scene wouldn't be acting,
and that caught her like a kick.

She made it a point to put her glass down before
turning back to him. "Thank you for the carriage,
Matt," she said, smiling a bit tremulously, trying very
hard to play the scene properly. "You spoil me terribly,
and I love every minute of it."

"My pleasure, darling." His voice was soft. Kelly
became very still, knowing what was coming and wondering if she hadn't had too much wine to handle it
well.

Matt reached out to touch her hair, watching it as
if he had discovered a treasure. "That light in your
hair is like the sparkle of jewels. I should have gotten
you topaz and diamonds to wind up in it."

He was doing it again. She'd been so comfortable,
so at ease with him. But the humor had faded completely in his eyes, and in its place Kelly found longing, arousal, affection. Just the sight of it, that and the
whisper of his fingertips against her hair, and she was
undone.

It didn't matter that this was supposed to be a
game played for the benefit of a stranger. She wanted
him. She wanted him to lace his fingers in her hair
and pull it loose. To feel his hands against her skin,
building her passion like the movement of a
symphony.

The impact of that discovery—something that had
never happened with such brutal intensity to her before—threatened her composure. She closed her eyes
for a moment in defense.

Matt gently pulled her to him. He bent to find her

lips and searched them with small exploratory kisses as he wound his arms about her. The feel of his hands against the bare skin of her back struck her like a shock. She jumped against him, a small sound of surprise caught in her throat. He only pulled her closer, folding her into the vise of his embrace until the buttons of his shirt made their imprint against her chest. It seemed that their hearts beat of the same accord, that for just a moment, they were what they pretended.

"The hell with the opening," he whispered huskily, tickling her neck with his lips. "Let's go home."

Kelly let her fingers rove in among his short rich hair, enjoying the soft, full feel of it. Tracing her hand along his temple, she outlined his ear with her thumb and then reached up to kiss it. Far in the back of her mind she knew that a powerful car idled nearby, waiting for them to finish the scene so they could continue on down to the riverfront.

She kissed Matt again, tasting the salt of his perspiration, and recognized that her own frightening arousal was more than reciprocated. Again the urgent pressure of his mouth parted her lips, a bruising, heady kiss, and she met his tongue with her own, only briefly, for its delight threatened to overwhelm her.

"No," she scolded breathlessly, pulling back as far as she could, unable to look away from the liquid yearning in his eyes. "They're expecting you, love. We'll get home later." Then because she couldn't help it, she reached up with her index finger and traced, slowly, the outline of his lips, so soft and sensitive, as if sealing their memory forever. "We'll go home later."

The big car that waited for them belonged to the owner of a chain of local movie houses. Matt and Kelly rode the rest of the way to the premiere with the little balding man and his once-handsome wife who'd long since traded what natural beauty she'd had for cosmetics and an overzealous plastic surgeon.

All the way there they poured champagne and gushed about their luck at having Matt Hennessy attend the premiere. It had been planned as a highlight of the social season, and every name in town had promised to show up for the benefit of the Heart Association. But since Matt had agreed to be on hand for the occasion, additional guests had come out of the woodwork, enthusiastically donating top dollar for the privilege of mingling with the star and his new lady. The Heart Association was grateful, the theater owner was grateful and St. Louis was grateful.

The non-stop monologue washed over Kelly like the lulling cadence of a ritual chant. The champagne was making mincemeat of the wine, and she was beginning to drift drowsily. There, somewhere halfway to sleep, was where she kept the dusty remnants of her dreams locked away, and here it was that they seemed still possible. It didn't seem terribly unreasonable to think that she could go with Matt to the premiere tonight and enjoy herself without suffering any consequences. She could just worry about those tomorrow.

It took no more than fifteen minutes to reach the impressive line of limos that stretched along Wharf Street. It was a gorgeous night, with the huge harvest moon just edging above the river. To their left the lights of the Eads bridge arched gracefully above their reflection. Beneath it the last of the riverboats still in existence gathered: *Lt. Robert E. Lee, Belle Angeline, Sam Clemons, Goldenrod.* And finally, the *Delta Queen,* her lights glittering like bright stars off the water. Kelly could hear the music coming from the boats, ragtime with its tinny pianos and banjos. Crowds strolled along the wharf, their attention torn between the spectacle of wealth that collected there and the even more impressive sight of the dull silver polish of the arch as it swept up over the night.

The decks of the *Delta Queen* bristled with designer labels and animal pelts. Kelly found herself hard-pressed at first to keep from gaping. The organizers had laid out a memorable party with an enticing buffet in the grand lounge and at least two different jazz bands for entertainment. Formal butlers cruised the rooms with well-laden trays, apparently instructed to let no hand remain empty. Even as the first group of official greeters approached to offer welcome, Kelly found a drink in her hand. Matt took hold of her arm supportively, not about to let her face the greedy eyes and questions without his help.

He needn't have worried. Kelly found that she had little trouble drifting in and out of different groups with or without Matt at her side. To her surprise as much as the people she met, she found that she was perfectly comfortable with them. She didn't shop at Saks or belong to any of their country clubs, but she was well-educated, and she found that she had heretofore undiscovered talent for adaptation. She thought Missy would be proud of the good time they were having.

After a while Matt finally got her away to himself. "You're a natural, kid," he said, holding her hand on his arm with his other hand as he steered her toward the door. "You have everybody eating out of your hand."

"Pretty heady stuff," she agreed, smiling over to two women she'd talked to earlier. "Now I know how Cinderella felt when she faced the prince's family."

Kelly let Matt lead her through the room and up

the steps to the top deck where one of the bands played to the outside crowd that had gathered there. They chose a bench at the far end of the deck and sat in the shadow of a smokestack. Before them the river glided by like molten pewter in the bright moonlight, and only a few stars were bold enough to be visible in the sky.

"I bet you arranged this, too," Kelly accused, indicating the breathtaking beauty of the night.

The band went into a wailing rendition of the St. James Infirmary Blues that made Kelly want to move. She finished her champagne and set the glass down, then leaned against Matt. The night breeze was chilly against her bare arms and back. Matt quickly slipped an arm around her and settled her against his chest.

"So tell me the truth," he said, propping his feet on the side railing. "How do you like the ball?"

Kelly considered a moment. "Not as formidable as I thought. This is a great crowd for crows."

Matt chuckled into her hair and leaned back, unconsciously rubbing her arms with his warmer hands. Kelly was afraid for a moment that she would become aroused, but all she felt was comfort—ease. She felt as if she were home.

"Do you go to this sort of thing all the time?" she asked.

"Not as much as people think," he said. "I spend most of my time avoiding publicity."

She couldn't help but grin. "Yeah, I can tell what a good job you do."

"It's rough work," he insisted, his voice amused. "The last time I was on the Academy Awards, I presented with Raquel Welch. Nothing more. By the next week, every rag in the country decided that she was having my baby."

Kelly grinned. "Oh, I think it'd be cute, with her red hair and your green eyes. What are you going to call it?"

"You know, I think you could be a real trouble-maker if you get the chance."

She could tell that he was smiling. She almost turned to see the tiny lines appear along his eyes and the dimples crease his cheeks. His teeth probably flashed in the moonlight. She laughed at that thought.

"What's so funny?" he demanded.

"Nothing." She giggled, looking up to see that his teeth did at least gleam. He was incredibly handsome in the gentle light of the moon, and Kelly was very glad she was with him. "I haven't had this much champagne since my wedding, and I'm afraid I'm going to get very silly any minute now."

"You go right ahead," Matt encouraged with a pleased grin. "I think I'd like to see you silly."

"Mr. Hennessy?" A breathless young woman appeared before them in a shimmering silver gown. It had obviously been airbrushed on and made Kelly's eyebrows raise of their own accord. She would look ridiculous in something like that. She'd look even sillier in the color of hair the woman had chosen. Kelly allowed herself a bright smile of greeting that only seemed to make the young woman lose her own.

"Yes?"

Matt straightened. Kelly was astonished at how quickly Matt assumed his stage persona. She could actually feel the tension rise in him as he created it. In a split second, although he seemed the same, he was someone she didn't know.

"The movie's about to start." The woman sounded as if she'd just completed the Boston Marathon.

Matt flashed her a smile that seemed to be just for

her and then turned back to Kelly. "C'mon, Kelly old girl, let's go pay for dinner." He eased her to her feet where it seemed that the boat was rocking a bit more than before.

More champagne greeted the moviegoers. Kelly was beginning to think that her liver would never survive a constant dose of this life-style. She entered the plush red theater on Matt's arm and smiled with honest delight when they were given a standing ovation. Jewels glittered in simulated gaslight and sleek heads nodded and smiled as she passed. Matt took special care to get her to her seat with a kiss before he took the stage for a brief speech to introduce the movie.

"I tried to get Kelly up here to show her off for you," he told the audience, hands in pants pockets to illustrate the famous informality, "but she doesn't seem to share my need for the public attention."

Kelly shot him a "you're pushing it again" look and smiled politely while the people around her murmured over her. It just amazed her that these same people who wouldn't know her from a grocery clerk any other day, fawned all over her as if she were a princess when she was on Matt's arm.

"He actually threatened to expose my work in the massage parlor if I tried to get up there with him," she said dryly to the matron next to her.

The lady in question, not exactly sure how to take Kelly's humor, simply pretended not to hear.

"Kelly's taken on the job as my personal guide to the area," Matt continued, his congeniality as picture perfect as a Rockwell illustration. "I have to admit now in public that until I met her, I had no idea what a wonderful place St. Louis was. She has every right to be proud of it. I've had a marvelous time in your lovely city, and so I'm more than happy to be able to donate a little time back by being here tonight."

The audience couldn't have been happier if Matt had said that he was inviting them all to his house for coffee.

~

KELLY HAD no idea what time they finally headed home. The boat docked around one, after the end of the elaborate buffet, but the party hardly took breath. The bands changed, and after dinner there was dancing. For quite a while Kelly had a lot of trouble getting a chance to dance with Matt. He was, of course, in demand, but she hardly ever waited by the punch bowl. Matt finally ended up having to cut in on a well-known divorce lawyer and then refused to let Kelly dance with anyone else.

Matt was a wonderful dancer. Kelly knew she shouldn't have been all that surprised, but she was delighted anyway. She'd never met a man who could dance with that effortless grace that made it a pleasure. Long ago Kelly had decided that Fred Astaire was an alien, since no one could dance like him. If so, Matt was from the same planet.

The crowd that gathered in the ballroom wasn't alone in being impressed by the elegant picture Matt and Kelly made on the dance floor. It made Kelly absolutely breathless. Matt held her close as they swept gracefully around. She loved the way Matt caressed the small of her back with his pleasantly rough fingers. She loved the pressure of his chest against her cheek and the way she fit so snugly against him. And she couldn't seem to get away from the heady aroma of his cologne.

When the band finally stopped playing, she would have paid them herself to keep on going. Even without the pleasant high the champagne had given her, she thought she would have known just how Eliza Doolittle felt. After spending an evening in Matt's arms, she couldn't think of anything she'd rather do.

They said good-bye to the other guests and set off in Estelle and Murray's limo, tired and satisfied with the way the party had gone. Kelly sat cradled in Matt's arms, humming along with him the last few songs they'd danced to, content to never move again. She was quite sure that if ever in her life she'd glowed, it was at that moment.

"Just let me off with Kelly," Matt said as they reached her house. "I left my car here."

As Kelly stepped out onto her sidewalk she took a slow, deep breath of night air to settle the more-than-champagne induced tingling in her limbs.

"You did not leave your car here," she accused Matt.

"They know that," he grinned, taking her purse to search for her key. "Great for the image. I'll sleep on the couch."

"You're asking an awful lot," she admitted truthfully.

The sound of their voices woke a few indignant night birds. Matt opened the door and ushered Kelly in.

"Hey, look." He led her over to where a bottle of Cabernet Sauvignon sat out on the coffee table. "It's from Missy. I'll open it."

"Missy?"

He handed her the note. It said simply, *I couldn't leave a white wine unchilled, and chances are you wouldn't have gotten as far as the ice box.* Kelly snorted unkindly and bent to slip off her high heels. The feel of the cool wooden floors against her hot feet was heavenly.

Matt opened the wine and handed her a glass as he undid his tie with his free hand. "C'mon. Let's go sit."

Kelly pulled up her stockinged feet to rub at them while she sipped a drink she certainly didn't need. Matt slipped out of his coat and sat next to her, unbuttoning the stiff collar of his formal shirt.

"Don't forget to take this jewelry back," she admonished, wishing he didn't have to. The sapphires gleamed up at her like a night sky, the diamonds its stars. She took one more sip of wine and then set it on the end table before turning back to face Matt again. "Thank you for tonight."

He smiled down at her, slipping his arm behind her on the couch. "It was all my pleasure. You showed everybody up just like I predicted. Besides, it was the least I could do since I'm letting you in for a battering from the press."

"Oh, they haven't been all that bad. The only real problem I've had has been with my supervisor. She's convinced that you're going to show up at the hospital one of these days and ravage me right there."

He grinned, and the dimples creased his cheeks. Kelly wanted to kiss them. "The national press won't pick up on it till Monday when the magazines come out," he assured her. "That's when you'll really be in for it."

She hadn't considered that. "You didn't warn me, you know."

"You wouldn't have come along." He took a drink of wine and leaned his head back a little as he savored it. "You know, it might not be a bad idea for you to get away for a week or two. Maybe you'd miss the brunt of it."

Kelly scowled, reaching over for just one more sip. "I'm a working stiff, pal. I can't just take off when the mood strikes me."

"Don't you have any vacation coming?"

"It's already scheduled for Christmas. I'm going to Colorado."

He nodded, going after more of the wine he'd set on the table. Kelly wondered how much it took to make him silly. He'd certainly partaken of his share that evening.

"Your family there now?" he asked easily.

"No."

Her answer was curt, abrupt, and it made her angry. She was being impolite for a slight he didn't mean. He didn't know about Kelly and Christmas—what it did to her to see the familiar memory-strewn streets of St. Louis adorned in holiday trimmings. Matt didn't know how much she'd hoped that Michael might have been able to dispel the ghosts of her past. But he had only added his own for her to deal with.

"No," she tried again, more evenly. "I go skiing over Christmas. Missy and I." Missy's family had never cared and Kelly really had no family to care. So, the two of them ran away every year.

"What about your family?"

Kelly felt herself stiffen. Why was that so important to him? It wasn't his business. It wasn't anyone's business. She wished she could take another drink of wine, that it might relieve the tight pressure of her guilt.

When she turned to answer, she flashed Matt what she hoped was no more than a rueful smile. "I think it's probably more than you bargained for in our deal,

Matt. And not something I handle well when I've been drinking."

"So it was more than Michael," he said quietly, very little surprise in his voice. "Kelly?"

She purposefully turned away from the pain mirrored in his eyes. More than Michael. Well, he was right there. It was just that she hadn't allowed herself to even think about it since Michael's death, except in the safe confines of Dr. Martinson's office. But somehow it seemed as if Matt had the right to garner those moments from her past that had made her the rigid, careful woman he had sought to free. He'd long since broken through her protective armor to the vulnerable core beneath, and yet had never tried to hurt her for it. She couldn't think he would be any different with this.

Rubbing her forehead to ease the pain, she found herself telling him. She could feel his concern like a warmth against her cheek. Like a gentle caress, his caring seemed to ease open old doors. "I was in nurses' training, and had to work nights. It was New Year's Eve, and Mom and Dad had taken the car to a local church dance." Edna and Francis, salt of the earth, saving scrupulously throughout their adult lives to send Kelly to private school and college, to give her what they hadn't had. Her father had been a policeman, a sergeant in the city, and had called her Macushla after an old Irish song. Her mother had kept house and had lost two babies before Kelly. She'd never quite lost her sorrow for the children she would never watch grow up. Edna and Francis had taught Kelly to take pride in what she did.

She stared now at her empty glass, its rim winking like the diamonds at her wrist. "They were late and hurried home so I could be on time for work. A drunk broadsided them at the corner." She'd heard the sirens and run to help, never expecting that it would be her parents they would pull out of the twisted wreck. "My mother died in my arms." Like Michael. "My father survived. He's, uh, remarried. A lovely lady with a big bunch of kids. They live in Chicago where his family's from."

Matt's voice was incredibly soft. "Your father blamed you?"

She shrugged uncomfortably. "Without realizing it, I guess. He had to blame somebody. He'd loved my mother since he was twelve."

Since that time, Christmas had become no more than brutal loneliness and unreasoning guilt. She'd thought that she could overcome it with Michael, that his compassion could heal her. But he'd died too, and it had only become worse. Since then, she'd just given up.

"Michael died near Christmas, too?"

Kelly couldn't imagine a gentler voice. She nodded blindly, rigid in his tender embrace. "Two days after. You're lucky you didn't show up in December. I tend to be a real drag then."

She didn't even know that a sob had caught in her throat until Matt took her face and gently turned it to him. His smile was so very gentle, his sea-green eyes searching out the anguish in her own.

"All right," he said quietly, "it's all out. I won't step in the wrong place and hurt you again, Kelly. I promise. I won't hurt you again."

Kelly realized that his eyes were more gentle than his voice or even his touch. Within their gaze she felt the old pains bubble out like poisons that had been held in too long. He was so close, the softly shaded green of his eyes liquid for the pain he shared with her. And yet when he smiled down at her, she felt that she could immerse herself in him and come away stronger.

Matt moved his hand and caught her face carefully in it. Bending to kiss one cheek and then the other, he collected her tears. Kelly sat very still, a now familiar tension beginning to ease the other way. She could feel the touch of his hands like healing fire. She closed her eyes and turned to find the soft strength of his lips. Again, instinctively, she reached out to him, her hand to his heart, to find his heart as if seeking the very core of him. She could feel the taut lines of his chest, and against her fingers the soft, curling hair that marked the hollow of his throat. Contact with him awakened her, her senses heightened as the current of touch coursed through her. She opened her lips to taste the delicious warmth of his skin, drinking in the sweetness of his comfort. It was as if he brought her back to life, and she suddenly thought that she needed that desperately.

Matt moved to her slowly, carefully, his lips searching her eyes, her cheeks, her throat. He kissed her ears and with one movement, undid her hair. It tumbled around her, the curls falling well past her shoulders. When he kissed her again, he tangled his fingers in it, stroking it like a precious silk. With one finger, he drew a line from her ear along her throat. He then kissed her shoulder, her arm, slowly, carefully, as if memorizing the taste and texture of it.

Kelly embraced his shoulders, trying to capture their breadth in her small hands, then ran her fingers over the tight muscles that strained against the linen of his starched shirt. She soaked in his vitality and tasted his excitement. Drawn by it, she bent to his throat, kissed the hollow there, wishing she could nestle against the haven of his chest. She stroked his chest, drinking in the sinewy strength of it, then found the flatness of his belly.

"Kelly," he whispered into her hair, his tongue teasing at her ear. "Oh, Kelly."

His one hand held her against him. The other caressed her gently, almost reverently. He explored her back, exciting chills up and down to the very small of it where he let his fingers play. And when he'd finished there, he carefully slid the dress down. His fingers brushed against the bare skin of first one shoulder, and then the other.

For the first time in two years, she allowed herself to experience the joy of a man's touch, the sweet pain of sharing a message more intimate and special than any other in the world. His tenderness brought fresh tears, and his arousal a thrilling elation. She thrilled to the pleasure like no other she'd ever known. She wanted Matt to consume her, to find the smallest parts of her and make them his.

He kissed her, his tongue running along her lips and in to meet her tongue, his hand caressing her throat. It felt as if he was almost afraid to touch her, so tantalizingly light was the contact. His fingers traced patterns along her shoulders, in the contours there, along the ridge of her collarbone, following them with deliberate ease. And then down. Discovering the exquisitely sensitive skin of her breasts, his touch setting her on fire. He circled her nipples to tingling rigidity with slightly rough fingers, and then gently kneaded the soft flesh within the grasp of his hand.

Kelly closed her eyes against the fierce yearning his touch ignited in her, a pain that pierced her belly like a hot knife. She felt as if she were a pliable instrument of pleasure in Matt's sure hands. When she opened her eyes, she saw his dark, tousled head bend to take her breasts. It was all she could do to keep from crying out. The long-forbidden desire he had unleashed battled in her chest with the sweet soreness of knowing that there was nothing in the world she wanted more than for Matt to make love to her. She felt stabs of pleasure as he took the taut nipple in his teeth, and arched against him, her head back. He sought her with his hands, their touch delicious against the velvet of her dress. His lips and tongue and teeth teased at her breasts until the sweet ache of it seared her to moving.

"Oh, God, Kelly," he whispered, his beautiful face nestled against her. "I want you. I want to be the one to take the pain from your eyes."

Kelly couldn't believe it. Matt's words, so sincere and full of emotion, set off a violent reaction in her. She stiffened abruptly, her eyes stark, her mouth wide with the effort to breathe. He couldn't. Dear God, he couldn't say that. It was bad enough that she realized she was falling in love with him. It would be catastrophic if he thought the same.

"Kelly?"

She saw the pain in his eyes, the confusion, and pulled away from him.

CHAPTER 8

"K elly, what's wrong?"

"Matt," she stammered, arms across her bare breasts as if warding off attack. "Please don't. Don't say things like that."

"What," he retorted quietly, his eyes giving her no room, "that I care for you?"

She shook her head, not ready to face him. "It's a game. We're playing a game, remember?"

Carefully, as if dealing with a frightened child, Matt reached out to her, his hand finding the tears that remained on her cheek. "I don't think so, Kelly. Not anymore. But I don't want to hurt you. God knows you've had enough of that."

He was silent for a moment so that Kelly was forced to face him, his gaze so understanding that it brought fresh tears.

"I'm sorry—" he smiled "—I surprised myself, too. I'll try to be more careful from now on and let you take the lead. We'll be friends. You let me know when you're ready for more."

His beautiful face blurred beyond the tears. Kelly

wasn't sure if she was more frightened or guilty for the hurt she'd seen in his eyes.

"What if that's never, Matt?" she had to ask.

He smiled at her with a small shake of his head. "Not possible. You have too much courage. And I have too much patience."

That at least brought a grin. "You? You're about as patient as the IRS on April fourteenth."

"Well—" he grinned right back "—at least you haven't lost your tact." Then brushing a stray lock of hair from her forehead, he bent to kiss it. "Now, my dear, don't you think you should be getting some sleep? You have to get to work in a while."

She faced him with as much courage as she could muster. "Would you mind if I just stayed here?"

Matt's answer was simply to take her back into his arms, her head against his chest, his hand against her hair. Kelly closed her eyes with the peacefulness of his embrace and found herself wishing she could stay forever.

When the phone rang, Kelly started from the easy sleep she was succumbing to. She felt Matt jump, his body tensing quickly.

At the second ring her heart lurched, an uncomfortable residue of the sudden frights of her life. "Who could be calling at this hour?" she demanded, her voice unconsciously harsh. Matt had already reached back to answer it.

"What do you mean, 'Oh, my God,' Missy?" he was asking. "We just got back." He didn't say another word into the phone as he handed it across without changing his hold on Kelly. "It's your fairy godmother."

"What's wrong?" Kelly greeted her friend without

preamble, unable to keep pictures of Missy injured or sick from her mind.

"Evidently nothing at all," Missy sang with undisguised glee.

"Missy, why are you calling me in the middle of the night?"

"Think again, kid. Have you bothered to look out the window lately? Or at a clock? No, on second thought, that's a dumb question. If Matt Hennessy were next to me in bed, I wouldn't look much farther, either."

"We're on the couch," Kelly retorted.

"Oh, great. A man with imagination. He just keeps getting better and better, doesn't he? I can hardly blame you for being late. Good thing I thought to call before Dragon Lady got here."

"You're really going to be embarrassed when I talk to you," Kelly threatened, knowing it was useless. "And what do you mean late? We just..." For the first time, she noticed the windows. The shapes of familiar shrubbery were becoming recognizable outside. It was beginning to get light. "Oh, my God."

"That's about the size of it. It's now edging past 6:50. You're due here in ten minutes."

Hardly taking the time to say good-bye, Kelly threw the phone back to Matt and was on her feet in one movement. "Matt, I'm late. Go on up and get some sleep. I'll turn off the phone, and I can take you home when I get back from work."

Reassembling her dress without a thought, she ran off to shower and slip back into her work persona. Hair carefully French-braided out of the way, makeup washed clean, she exchanged her jewelry for gold post earrings and a class pinky ring.

The sapphires winked richly up at her as she palmed them, ready to take them back to Matt. She'd slipped them off with palpable regret, not wanting to let go of the fairy tale they represented. The woman in the mirror this morning, though, wasn't the same one who'd sported these last night. She'd just slip them onto Matt's dresser as she walked by his room.

As she walked by, she saw that the door was still open. Matt was already in bed, but still awake. For just the briefest of moments when she saw him, Kelly froze. The movie they'd seen the night before had had a scene in which Matt's character had laid in bed, but still awake, just like now, waiting for the heroine to arrive. The sense of déjà vu momentarily threw her off. His smile was unconsciously identical.

"You look different again," he said, slipping his arms beneath his head. She wished he'd at least kept his shirt on. The sight of him ignited fresh memories and emotions.

"I wanted to give you the jewelry," she answered quietly. "If I don't give them back now, I may never do it at all."

"Well, then, before I go, we'll have to get you a set of your own."

"No, we won't."

His smiled gentled. "It's just my way of saying thank you for making me a new man. You're worth every carat."

She smiled in return, giving mischief for mischief. "Carrots, now there's a great idea. They're great for the eyesight and they don't ruin your figure."

His answering smile was complacent, as if the question were already settled. "Have a good day at work."

Kelly turned to leave, but paused for just a moment and found herself facing him again. "Matt," she said, not speaking about the gala she'd been able to attend and knowing that he understood. "Thank you."

Before he could answer, she closed the door and left.

Sometimes it was nice that the hospital was twenty minutes from her house. Driving was always a favorite time for her to meditate on life in general and soak in the often beautiful scenery. Sometimes when the mood was on her she sang along with the radio.

Then again, there were times like now, when the twenty minutes seemed to stretch into agonizing days. She was late, which was rare, but if there was one thing Sister Agatha considered unforgivable, it was tardiness.

After all the publicity about Kelly's situation and the nun's obviously jaundiced attitude to the whole supposed affair, Kelly could imagine the reception she would be accorded upon her hasty arrival. The fact that by now Missy would have undoubtedly announced the exact circumstances in which she'd found Kelly would no doubt worsen the situation considerably. She could hardly wait.

Gnawing at her even more than the situation she rushed toward was the one she'd just left behind. The careful equilibrium she'd built so assiduously the past two years was fast disintegrating. In the period of only a few days, Matt had ignited emotions more powerful than she'd ever known and resurrected the enthusiasm she'd so deliberately shut away. He made her want to sing, to run out and taste the world as if she'd never seen it before. When she saw that mad, mischievous spark in his eyes, she wanted to follow along just to see what he'd pull next. And after he had held her in his arms and absorbed the pain she'd exposed to him, she realized that she always wanted it to be his arms she sought for solace. For the first time since Michael died, she wanted to celebrate her life.

Matt had said that she had courage. Did she? Did she really have the guts to try again? It was so hard to separate the excitement from the fear, that she wasn't sure. Maybe she should run like hell from his bright, laughing eyes and understanding smile before she ended up with another load of grief to carry around. The more he woke the dormant life in her, the more he stirred the fires of dread. Kelly just wasn't sure she could handle it.

At least where it counted in immediate terms, her luck seemed to run hot that day. Kelly made it to work by 7:40 and escaped to breakfast before Sr. Agatha even made it in. Everyone looked at her as if she'd just had lunch with the president, so she figured that Missy had indeed enlightened them all concerning the phone conversation. Kelly got back at her smug friend by outright refusing to answer anyone's questions about anything that happened after she and Matt had arrived home. Every time the questioning got too near the limit, she just smiled to herself as if remembering something very nice and shook her head. She knew that she was letting herself in for harassment, but figured it was driving them all, especially Missy, nuts.

Within an hour, the entire hospital had the news that Matt Hennessy was at Kelly's house, and that Missy's call had interrupted their unbridled passion at a most inopportune moment. Sister Agatha missed everything but the giggling and round eyes of appreciation that greeted each new telling of the story.

Rich got the house staff's elaborated-upon version sometime before lunch. Kelly knew that, because of the hurt-puppy eyes he greeted her with when she saw him in the cafeteria. She saw that and realized instinctively that her problems had somehow been compounded without her even knowing about it.

"Would you mind being seen with a reluctant celebrity?" she greeted him wryly as she set her tray across from him and sat down. Eyes everywhere followed her as she moved, and she didn't like it, accurately reading the disapproval.

"You sure you want to sit with me?" he asked back, his smile sincere. "The entire staff over there is watching you like you're Mary Magdalen."

Kelly snorted rather unkindly and picked up her fork to eat. "People amaze me. They know you and I have been friends for two years. They also know that Matt and I haven't. Says a lot for the power of suggestion."

Kelly rubbed a little at the grit in her eyes and thought that this was the second time since she'd met Matt that she'd forfeited a night's sleep. Bad habit to get into. Then she realized how very quiet Rich had gotten. Putting her hand down, she scrutinized his downcast eyes and saw the pain. Damn, she thought with a sinking feeling, I wasn't wrong after all. Something was going on here.

"Rich?"

He looked up, doing his best to look noncommittal.

"What's wrong?"

He shrugged a little stiffly, his eyes having trouble staying locked into hers. "Nothing, Kelly."

"Nothing, hell," she retorted, leaning forward a little. "Come on, Rich, we're friends. What's wrong?"

Then he looked at her, and Kelly felt her heart hit her feet. There was no mistaking that look.

"We're not friends?" she asked very carefully, her voice gentle.

His smile when he answered was rueful. "You're friends, Kel. I've been more than that for a while."

"Oh." She couldn't think of anything helpful to say. "Oh, Rich, I—"

His hand came up. "Kelly, don't. I know how you feel, and that's okay. I'm sure that if you never come to regard me in a different light that I'll survive just fine. I didn't want you to know because I was afraid you, uh, wouldn't want to see me again."

"Well I don't want to hurt you."

He smiled again, his soft brown eyes tender. "You'd hurt me a lot more if you didn't consider me your friend anymore. Okay?"

Kelly didn't realize that the torn empathy in her eyes sealed Rich's heart for good. She nodded, though, which helped broaden his smile. It only made her feel slightly better.

BY THE TIME the shift ended, Kelly felt like a zombie, hardly able to keep her stinging eyelids open. All she wanted to do was drag her body home and get some sleep after a marathon hot bath.

She'd just finished admitting a patient when she ran into one of the evening nurses with the afternoon paper. In the society column was a picture of Kelly entering the theater on Matt's arm, and Kelly had to admit it was impressive. The reaction from the staff this time got so noisy that Sister Agatha materialized in the work lane like the avenging angel. The look in her eyes was enough to shatter glass.

"Miss Byrne," she enunciated icily, "just when do you think you will allow my emergency room to return to normal?"

"Sister," Kelly admitted truthfully as she refrained from rubbing at her sleep-starved eyes, "I would be more than happy to see that happen right now."

Eight heads turned with the conversation, unsure just how to react or whether it was wise to react at all.

"Then I can assume that the gentleman in question will be gone soon?"

"In about a week."

Again the heads turned for the nun's answer.

Sister Agatha's look would have sent a lesser person diving for cover. By now Kelly was used to it. "Another week like the one we have had would be unthinkable. I suggest you tell Mr. Hennessy to go home now."

She never even thought to wait for an answer before turning to leave. Kelly felt a rare blush staining her cheeks.

"You tell him to leave before I've met him," a nurse hissed in her ear, "and your life would be meaningless."

Ten minutes later, Kelly was in the process of trying to report off to the evening shift when Dolly Inge, the triage secretary pulled up to a screeching stop right before her.

"He's here," she said panting, her eyes wider than they were the time the chief surgical resident mooned her at the front desk.

"Who's here?" Kelly automatically asked, her mind on the two patients she was handing over to Liz Parker, her replacement.

When Dolly echoed an incredulous, "*Who's* here?" Kelly knew. Her head jerked up as if on the end of a string.

"He wouldn't."

"You can't believe it," the secretary gasped, completely at a loss. "I was standing there telling Ella about how my kids, you know, Jeff and Erin, had to go to the doctor for their ears, when he just walked up—Matt Hennessy—" Heads turned, and the crowd began to reform. "Just walked up to my desk and said hello, just like that. Oh God, I'm shaking all over."

"Good thing he didn't ask her name," Missy muttered dryly. "She might have dropped dead on the spot."

"Where is he?" Kelly demanded, ignoring Missy.

"You're just not going to believe it," Dolly insisted, eyes even wider.

"We heard that part already," Kelly reminded her. "Get on with it before we break out the bamboo shoots."

Dolly looked around her as if daring anyone to dispute her word. "He's in Sister Agatha's office."

"You're lying," Missy retorted.

Everyone else beat tracks for the nearest mirror, which left Missy, Kelly and Liz to get a stealthy peek in the supervisor's office. Kelly almost choked. Matt was indeed there, smiling his most disarming and sincere smile as if he'd heard Sister's latest directive about him. And the supervisor, who some insisted had teethed on iron ore, was smiling back like a seventy-year-old schoolgirl, eyes and hands all aflutter.

"I wonder when she pours tea," Missy sneered.

"It would be so nice if he'd warn me once in a while," Kelly muttered blackly.

"Oh my God," Liz breathed, absolutely frozen at the sight of Matt.

Kelly wondered where he had just been. He was in blue slacks and a heavy cream sweater that made him look like a ski instructor. Totally without consent, she felt that rush of bittersweet emotion at the sight of him.

At that moment, Sister offered to take Matt out to see Kelly, and the conspirators were forced to flee. They made it back to the work lane in time to see six applications of fresh makeup, one set of entirely new scrubs and Sister and Matt approaching at the end of the hall.

Kelly groaned. Matt had another box under his arm.

"Hi, honey," he said, smiling at her, his eyes absolutely overflowing with delight at the sight of her. "Thought I'd drop in to surprise you."

Kelly was sure she heard sighs from behind her. Sister Agatha did nothing but beam, even when Matt dropped a quick kiss on Kelly's forehead to the sound of more sighs.

"You just like to disrupt my day, don't you?" she said with a smile. The next word was delivered as if the honey were in jeopardy of going rancid. "Darling?"

"That's because I know how big a kick you get out of it," he said, grinning back, his eyes negating the other people in the room. Kelly really wished that his gaze didn't attack her heart rate like it did.

"Yes—" she grinned mischievously, knowing full well that they had everyone's undivided attention "—it ranks right up there with power outages and nuclear war. What brings you here?"

"I figured that as late as we got in last night, I could

meet you here and drive you home. I'm glad I did. You look beat."

"Nobody can top Matt for a compliment," she said over to Liz, who was still trying to remember how to breathe.

"And guess what I found out?" he went right on, enjoying himself immensely. "Did you know that Saks is right on the way out here?" He held up a hand at her protest. "I know, I promised. But I just couldn't help it. You know what an impetuous guy I am."

They went through the whole act again, which, as tired as Kelly was, and after her conversation with Rich, threatened to throw her into overload. Matt bought the hospital off with a donation "To keep his favorite charity employed" and mesmerized her friends, effortlessly remembering their names as they sat over coffee in the lounge. He even stopped in to visit a couple of patients who had the good fortune to be injured that day.

Of course Kelly had to open the box, and of course inside lay a beautiful cream silk dress with low, rounded neckline and shirred half-length sleeves, tied at the waist with a Kelly green obi sash. It would look stunning on her, he knew, and oh, he forgot the small box with the diamond and emerald necklace and matching earrings he'd been unable to resist. After all, he'd added, those carats didn't do any damage to her figure, either, and they were certainly easy on his eyesight."

When he left with Kelly to drive her home, everyone envied her unspeakably. Matt grinned wholeheartedly at the success of his mission, and Kelly could have hit him.

He helped her in with eloquent flourish and folded himself behind the wheel, looking for all the world like a handsome, footloose heir about to run his small sports car along the Pyrenees mountains. His good-natured smile was so damn infectious and his chin incredibly square. And for the first time Kelly admitted how very empty her day was without him.

She leaned back against her seat and closed her eyes, the sting of frustrated tears taunting her. "Why did you have to put on such a production?" she demanded as Matt started the car and pulled out.

"Because otherwise you wouldn't have accepted the gifts," he answered easily. "You're like that, you know."

"Probably for a good reason," she retorted, eyes closed as she leaned her head back on the seat. "How come you're out on the prowl today anyway? I thought you had a schedule to keep."

"Oh, Meredith had something else to do today," he said with studied nonchalance. "Especially after we talked this morning."

Kelly's eyes were suddenly open again. She lifted her head and faced him. Matt kept his eyes on the road. The bright afternoon sunlight sought out the red highlights in his hair and paled the green of his eyes. Kelly thought she'd never seen a man so handsome or alive. That he cared for her at all brought the pain of new tears to her throat.

"We've decided to just be friends," he was saying out to the highway. Kelly thought she was beginning to hate the sound of that word.

He was smiling now, a self-deprecating edge to the dimples. "When I admitted to her that I was finding it more and more difficult to stay away from you, she just gave me a big 'I told you so' smile. She's said all along that she was much too conservative for a wild man like me."

There were a hundred things Kelly wanted to say. She wanted to tell Matt that in such a short time he couldn't be sure enough about her to give away a relationship he'd already established. That he shouldn't count on her enough to make that kind of choice. She couldn't manage. He was crowding her, unleashing the yearning that was so dangerous.

Matt looked over then, and saw the turmoil in Kelly's eyes. "I also told her that until you said differently, you and I were friends. I told you I wouldn't pressure you, and I meant it. I just didn't want to wait to tell Meredith what you made me understand—that as much as I care for her, she's been right all along. She's not the kind of woman I want to spend my life with. And I'm definitely not the man she needs in hers."

Matt had offered the last words to make Kelly feel better. They only served to further stir the maelstrom in her chest.

"Does this change your travel plans?" she asked, her voice sounding abrupt.

Matt looked over briefly again and then returned his attention to the highway. "Not at all. I have a week left before I have to leave for a movie location, and any number of functions I'm expected to attend. I fully intend to hold you to your bargain."

A week was going to last too long and pass much too quickly for her to be able to keep her wits when it came to Matt. How could she possibly be sensible when it came to a man who unleashed such emotions in her? How could she deal with the pleasure and joy he provoked when she was with him, and the dread when she was alone?

Kelly leaned back again in her seat and closed her eyes, the sounds of the traffic in rhythm with her slowly easing heartbeat. Even though Matt returned his attention to driving, Kelly felt his eyes on her from time to time and realized that he was enjoying the silent ride together as much as she.

That night after Matt had returned to his hotel, Kelly gratefully climbed into her bed, ravenous for the sleep she'd been missing and impatient for the release it afforded from the stress building up in her. She never got it. For the first time in almost a year, the nightmare returned.

CHAPTER 9

Matt had actually underestimated the repercussions of the national press. Monday morning Kelly's picture showed up in *People* magazine. By Tuesday less reputable tabloids had her pregnant and/or already married to Matt. She was labeled everything from nurse's aide to chief of cardiology at a major Midwest medical center.

Missy collected the articles to save for a scrapbook she was sure Kelly would want later. Sister Agatha posted a notice that no reporter would be allowed on the premises no matter what. She also flew in the face of one of the hospital administrators when he suggested that it might be better for the hospital if Kelly took an unpaid leave of absence until the publicity cooled a little. No one dared interfere with Sister's nurses, and since in her opinion Kelly was an excellent nurse whose work hadn't been affected—yet—the whole idea was dismissed as absurd.

In the end, the publicity was like a good news, bad news joke. The bad news was that Kelly was followed more closely than Jackie O. Her house was staked out, her every move photographed and analyzed by every less noteworthy press source of

the world. Soon, the only place she was able to find any peace was at work. And since it had never been busier or more demanding, the peace she found there was, to say the least, minimal.

Matt steadied her when she was with him, and Missy took over at other times. But by the end of the week Kelly had stopped trying to give Matt back the emeralds. She was beginning to believe that they were the least she deserved.

The good news was that Kelly was kept so frantically occupied that she had little time or energy to expend on the mounting toll her feelings for Matt were taking. At least she was occupied during the day. At night the fear bubbled up out of the irrational recesses of her subconscious, and resurrected the nightmares.

They were nothing she could remember. Nothing she could put a finger on. But four nights running, she woke sweating and shaking, an aftertaste of stale terror following her to consciousness.

She kept trying to put it down to stress. She hadn't had to deal with anything but work and housecleaning for so long that gearing up for this kind of circus act had sapped her reserves of stamina. It was good enough excuse if she really thought about it but not right now.

She knew, even as she tried to rationalize around it, that the stress was from falling in love again. Falling in love so precipitously that she had no way to break her fall. Matt had set her on fire, physically and emotionally. He had single-handedly returned to her the warmth and delight of the world around her that she'd put away in defense of her vulnerability. He had ignited emotions Kelly had never before experienced, highs and lows that frightened her for their vivid intensities. And in a life where Kelly had been blessed with the love of many generous and gentle people, Matt was the dearest and gentlest of all. But her emotions were threatening to overwhelm her in a way they never had before. She knew that if she really gave in to the feelings Matt was stirring up, and if she then lost him, she would lose herself.

The last day Matt was to spend with her dawned crisp and bright—football weather. A day for a horseback ride through the mountains, where autumn still flared majestically against the cerulean sky.

Kelly stretched luxuriously at her window, watching massive cotton ball clouds tumble over the horizon and thinking about the evening to come. Matt was intending to take her to Central West End for dinner and then a party in one of the palatial old homes nearby, another command performance for the adoring public. Tonight she would wear the emeralds and the soft silk dress Matt had bought her. She walked over to look at the gems again, just as she had all week, as if finding in them a symbol of her dilemma.

Again, the jewels had been simply crafted. The earrings were square-cut emeralds surrounded by small diamonds. The necklace showed a matching stone of deepest Ireland green that hung suspended from two arcs of diamonds and gold. All flattering, and well beyond anything Kelly would ever have dreamed of owning.

This time as she considered the jewels, glowing softly against the rich black velvet of the jewelry box, the tears she'd held off all week filled her eyes and spilled onto the gems like raindrops on exotic flowers.

Matt would surely expect some kind of commitment to a relationship that had begun only two weeks ago. And Kelly would again have to try and explain the burden of the nightmare and long years spent in the company of guilt and loss. She would have to make him realize that emeralds were a precious gift that simply couldn't fit with the life she'd managed to salvage. Too precious and too rare to waste on someone still too afraid to appreciate them as they deserved.

With a push she snapped the jewelry box closed. It was time to clean the house. She hadn't gotten much of a chance to do it the past couple of weeks, and today she desperately needed the mindless comfort of it. She wiped the tears with the back of her arm and turned from the room, her footsteps echoing endlessly before her as she walked down the hall.

An hour later, as she finished polishing the kitchen floor to a frantic gem-quality shine, the door-bell rang. At first she ignored it. She wasn't in the mood for company today. Her eyes were puffy and her temper short, the physical activity not doing her any good for once.

Her visitor tried again, and then again. Kelly pulled out her glass cleaner and went after the mirror in the hall, a large, gilt framed beauty she'd found for thirty dollars at an estate sale. The woman in it today scowled as she wiped, hair shoved unceremoniously up in a bandanna, eyes dark from sleeplessness. She'd awakened again the night before, and as usual had not been able to hold on to the dream.

As she rubbed, she heard a scratching at the back door. Probably Fritz, she thought, finishing the mirror with a swoop and then heading for the kitchen. She noticed that it was already noon. Time flies when you're having fun. She smiled sourly to herself and found that she had paused a moment to fight off a new threat of tears. Reaching in to put the glass cleaner away, she flipped open the back door with the other hand.

"C'mon in, Fritz. All you're getting today is lunch. I'm lousy company." Where was her furniture polish? She bent farther to search for it amid the jumble of aerosol cans and paper bags that populated the cabinet.

"I'm not Fritz, but can I still have lunch?"

Kelly cracked the back of her head when she jolted up in surprise. She'd forgotten to back out of the cabinet first. With a resounding thump, she sat heavily on the floor rubbing the back of her head. Standing almost at her feet, Matt rose in disproportionate height above her, grinning. He was in jeans and jacket, and looked as if he'd just come off a mountain trail somewhere.

Kelly tilted her head to the side, seeing the unusual lines of strain that pulled at his face. "Matt, I think I should tell you that not only is it not time for dinner, but you're not dressed for it."

He grinned with that self-assurance that sent Kelly's heart skidding. "Then it's a good thing we're going horseback riding instead."

She didn't move. "I'm cleaning."

Matt took a moment to consider the house. "Any cleaner and you could do surgery in here. Go horseback riding with me."

Kelly got to her feet and took her time putting away her rags before facing him again. "Matt, I really don't feel like it. This is the first day this week I've been able to blow my nose without making the national news, and I need it. Besides, I didn't sleep again last night."

"No problem," he said, his voice enthusiastic as his eyes melted with her last words. "I've arranged privacy. I even have a picnic lunch. Pâté and champagne."

He didn't understand, and she couldn't tell him. Just the sight of him so close, the sun warming his skin and lighting his hair, the faint scent of his after-shave mixing with the woodsmoke of autumn air sent her heart racing. She couldn't think to speak intelligently, couldn't muster the will to throw him out or make him stay. She just wanted some time to herself, to ease the terrible tension of what he was doing to her.

"I...can't." She turned away, looking for something in need of attention, finding nothing. "Matt, I'm a mess. I can't go out looking like this."

"C'mon," he insisted, taking her by the arm and propelling her toward the door. "The horses won't mind any more than I will."

A chauffeured limo sat at the curb, and before Kelly could protest Matt had her in the back seat and they were off.

"Didn't anybody tell you that it's easier to fool the press if you don't show up in this neighborhood in a limo all the time?" she teased, trying her best to work her way past the turmoil his nearness was setting off in her.

"Half the fun is the challenge. Set 'em up and then surprise 'em."

His voice still had that bright edge to it, but Kelly suddenly sensed a hardening to it. A purposeful feign. It made her see pain in him where none had been, and that set up an ache in her. She wanted to hold him. To ease the brittleness in his eyes with her touch.

"You want to tell me why you turned to a life of kidnapping?" she asked instead.

He watched the jewel-bright sky instead of her when she answered. "Pure impulse. I'm like that, you know."

"Baloney. Something happened. Something besides having to deal with a semi-psychotic nurse." She waited, but got no answer. "Matt?"

Matt finally faced her with wry amusement. "Why did I have to kidnap you? You're probably the only person around right now who would bother to harass me into telling you."

"In that case, you need a better class of friends. Spill it, pal."

He chuckled a little and relaxed back in his seat, a companionable arm over her shoulders. "What you see is pure frustration. It's been a long time since I haven't gotten my way. I've been on the phone all morning trying to wiggle my way out of the shooting date this week. I just found out that my mother has to have surgery, and I, uh, kind of wanted to be there."

"They're not going to let you?"

He shook his head, and Kelly saw the fear he didn't want to admit. "Iron clad. I'm off to the Arctic Circle first thing in the morning. Mom goes to the hospital Monday for surgery on a growth they found on her lung."

Now Kelly took his hand, her grip firm, and trapped his eyes with her own. Just as he'd accepted her pain and dread, she accepted his, the vulnerability that he finally allowed to show in his eyes.

"I'll be here if there's anything I can do," she said simply. "You know that."

His smile was grateful. "I know that, Kelly."

For a long moment they shared their silence, the support each could give the other. Then Matt squeezed Kelly's hand and drew her just a little closer, his eyes gently wry.

"If you're going to be here, does that mean you're not going to run off with me tomorrow?"

His words set off the pain again, the fire of yearning and fear. She tried to joke her way past it. "I don't have a thing to wear to meet Santa Claus, Matt."

He nodded, almost to himself, and reached up to trap a tear with his finger. "You probably don't even like the taste of whale blubber."

She grinned through the new tears. "I don't even like the sound of it."

"Well, my friend," he said, his eyes losing their humor, "I have some news for you. I've already fallen in love with you. I warned you that I'm an impulsive character."

The fire leaped high, searing her chest and heating her tears. She could hardly see the hypnotic green of his eyes for them.

"I don't know what to say, Matt. I hate the idea that you're leaving..."

He smiled, and she saw an understanding there she'd never found anywhere else. "But just the same, you're relieved." The smile broadened when she didn't protest. "I'm not blind, Kelly. I know what the pressure's been doing to you. It would have been more than most people could handle even without what you've lived through before."

She looked down at her hand, protected within the expanse of his. "I just keep wanting to run and hide," she admitted with a small shake of her head. "And that's no way to make a decision."

"Do you care for me?"

All she could manage was a nod.

He nodded back, satisfied. "All right, then we'll

just wait. I'm going to be out of touch until the new year with this movie. Why don't we plan to get back together then and start over from the beginning?"

"Are you sure?" she asked, facing him with her fear. "I may end up calling it quits after all."

"We'll deal with that in January," he said, smiling, his hand at her hair. "I care too much to force you someplace you don't think you can go. But I'll warn you now—" he grinned rakishly "—I'm a lucky guy. I always get what I want in the end. And Kelly, I want you." His eyes holding hers as tenderly as he held her hand, Matt bent to kiss her, as if sealing his words. "Now," he said a moment later, "let's enjoy the rest of our time together. No more talk of commitments. Okay?"

They spent that beautiful afternoon on a private estate that stretched along the rolling hills over-looking the Missouri River. The horses they rode were the finest, and they pushed them hard, racing, jumping hedges and then just walking along a lake where Canadian geese rested. They ate their picnic lunch in an English garden and played with the Great Dane who held court there. When the sun scattered brilliant rubies along the vast river, they climbed back into the limo and headed home.

Two hours later Kelly and Matt sat on her couch waiting for yet another limo to take them out for their last assignment. Matt was cleaned and pressed and handsomely masculine in tweed jacket and charcoal-gray slacks. Kelly, alongside, wore Matt's gifts, the emeralds winking darkly against the rich umber of her hair—as it fell from combs behind her ears. She was showered, and should have felt refreshed. Instead, she felt as if she were going to fall over. She was missing at least half of what Matt was saying. It took great effort to keep from rubbing at her eyes and smudging her makeup.

"Kelly," Matt finally said, "why don't you put your feet up for a few minutes?"

She shook her head, not seeing his gentle amusement. "I'm okay. The last thing you need is to be seen stuffing a limp body into a limo."

"Come on," he coaxed, drawing her closer with a protective arm. "The car won't be here for a while yet."

His voice was so soothing, and Kelly felt truly miserable. Maybe if she just curled up for a minute she'd feel better. She pulled her feet up next to her, and Matt eased her over so that her head rested in his lap.

"See?" He smiled down at her, stroking her hair with a gentle hand. "You fit perfectly."

"I'm custom-made for this couch," she mumbled, the comfort of his touch too much for her sleep-starved nerves. "I'm also..."

"Exhausted," Matt finished for her a moment later, his eyes incredibly wistful as he looked down at the deceptively fragile-looking woman in his arms.

When the chauffeur arrived ten minutes later, he was to find Matt Hennessy sitting very still on the couch, holding Kelly in his arms as if she were a sleeping child. An afghan covered her slight figure, and the perfect emeralds glittered at her ears. The chauffeur thought that it was too bad he had long since made a personal vow of secrecy about his clients. This was a picture everyone should see.

Kelly heard the violin and came awake with a start. When she tried to sit up, Matt's hold on her tightened.

"Oh, Matt," she apologized, "I'm sorry."

She blinked her eyes a couple of times to clear the sleep.

"For what?" he demanded, helping her to a sitting

position. "Working fifteen hours a day to satisfy the whims of a selfish movie actor? I'm the one who's sorry. I saw how tired you were and didn't do anything about it."

"But I..."

Still half asleep, Kelly struggled to pull all her senses together. She didn't quite manage. Noises from behind her caught her attention. Suddenly she found herself staring.

"Matt."

"Yes, Kelly."

"There's a man in my dining room playing the violin."

He looked over. "I know."

The man nodded, smiled and went on playing.

"He's wearing a tuxedo," she said. "Just like the three other men standing there."

Matt nodded. "That's what some waiters wear."

Now she turned to him. "That's not my china or crystal on the table."

"I know." He smiled passively. "It came with the waiters."

"But how did it all get here?"

"Well, when I canceled our plans for the evening, the chauffeur found himself with a free car and nothing to do. He went over and picked it all up."

She was still struggling for coherence while the four men watched in placid silence. "Dinner?"

"He brought that, too. Different restaurant. Everyone's been most delightful." Matt held out his arm. "Ready to eat?"

She looked around her again, at the violinist who was playing a Strauss waltz, at the three very elegant gentlemen by her staircase. She looked at her dining room table, covered in snow-white linen, Haviland china and Waterford crystal, long, tapered candles flanking a centerpiece of flowers. Then, because she could think of nothing else to do, she nodded. "Yes."

As they walked into the dining room, Kelly turned to the violinist. "Do you know 'Somewhere over the Rainbow'? Because I think I am."

He just smiled and instead went into a classicized version of "You're the Top."

"Matt," Kelly said as he held her chair. "You're expected at that party."

"They'll survive," he assured her, unfolding her napkin with a flair and spreading it across her lap. "It's my last night here, and I prefer to spend it with you."

"And Waiter's Local 360," she muttered under her breath with a sidelong glance.

"Besides," he said, quite unperturbed. "I wanted to be able to see you blow your nose in peace."

Her smile was dry. "You're too good to me."

He grinned right back from his place beside her. "I know."

Matt wasn't finished with surprises. When he nodded to the waiters, they bowed and turned for the kitchen. They quickly returned, laden with matching silver trays. Kelly took one look and burst out laughing. On each, carried as if they were the rarest of feasts, were a variety of cartons from a local Chinese takeout restaurant.

"Matt, how did you know?" she demanded when able to take a breath. The waiters began to calmly dish out the food as if it were their traditional chore.

"That Chinese was your favorite pig-out food?" Matt retorted with a bright grin. "Easy. I paged through your address book and found a disproportionate number of Chinese restaurants listed." He was served a can of beer, so he paused to pop and test it.

Then he nodded to the waiter who grinned and stepped back. "Besides, I also found Missy's number, and she verified it. Eat up. I can't wait to read the fortune cookie."

Kelly couldn't ever remember having a better time. They had beer with the appetizers, white wine with the Princess Chicken and red with the Beef and Broccoli. They were finally stuffed, and empty cartons littered the table as the violinist embarked on the second run-through of his repertoire. Matt poured them each a glass of plum wine and guided Kelly out for a walk.

The night was quiet. The streetlights broke through the latticework of the leaves and sketched patterns on the sidewalk. Kelly walked arm-in-arm with Matt trying to ignore the block-long limo that followed them along the street.

"I'm glad we didn't go tonight," Matt said, looking down at Kelly. "I didn't want to share you with anybody."

"You just wanted beer and Moo Shu Pork," Kelly said with a smile, their easy intimacy more poignant for Matt's leaving.

He shook his head, the humor gone. "I wanted to be with you, away from the pressure. You're beautiful tonight, Kelly." Stopping beneath a great old tree where the shadows were deepest, he drew her to him. "Do you know what the candlelight looked like in your eyes? Like sunlight on a lake, the fire against that blue. I'm going to miss that."

Don't say things like that, Kelly wanted to cry. I'm counting the hours until you leave, and they're dwindling so quickly. Don't make it worse.

Yet she couldn't look away from him. Her heart pounded in her throat and her breathing was made

even more erratic by the fear—and desire—he unleashed in her. She wished she could tell him how
much she loved him.

"Maybe I should have gotten you sapphires instead
of emeralds after all," he was saying, his hand testing
the soft texture of her hair.

She shook her head ever so slightly. "Too late. You
missed the deadline on expensive gifts."

He never moved, his eyes lost in shadow, his smile
drawing lines deeper in his cheeks. "So I did. I'll just
have to think of something else."

Before Kelly could think to protest, Matt bent to
kiss her, his hand still caught up in her hair. Guided
by instinct, the hot fire once again leaping in her, Kelly
stretched up to meet him. Eyes closed, arms up to his
shoulders, those huge strong shoulders that so overwhelmed her, she molded her body to the rock hard
planes of his. She had never tasted anything so sweet,
known a possession so total. He savored her as if she
were a rare and enticing wine, the dance of his tongue
against hers sending molten heat coursing through
her limbs. Kelly gave herself up to him, only wanting
the delicious communion of his touch.

Matt raised his head, his eyes still dark and un-
readable. "Let's go back, now, Kelly."

When they walked back into the house, all traces
of the impromptu dinner were gone, even the violinist.
Kelly couldn't help looking around, half expecting
them to be replaced by brownies. Her house was completely clean. Now it was just a matter of saying good-
bye to Matt.

He turned to her by the door and took her in his
arms. She saw in his eyes what the shadows had hidden. The love and the pain. The age-old look of a man
who had to leave.

"Let me know how your mom does," Kelly managed, her voice sounding tight even to her.

Matt nodded. "We'll talk in January."

Barely able to breathe now for the pain of his leaving, Kelly nodded back. "Take...care of yourself." Even saying the words sent a knife through her.

"I'll be back," he said simply. "With sapphires."

And then, very gently, he kissed her. His lips caressed hers with a tenderness that was agony, and his hands gently held her face. Kelly knew he tasted her tears. She lasted through the kiss and stood still as he walked to the door, knowing he didn't want to leave. She watched the rigid set of those shoulders and wanted to tell him not to go.

He'd opened the door, his coat in hand, his eyes, those incredible sea-green pools reflecting his struggle. His hand on the door, he stopped, and Kelly's heart raced.

"Oh, damn it."

When he turned, Matt trapped her eyes with his need. Kelly knew she had no choice. She held out her arms to him and he returned, sweeping her into his arms. Kelly gasped at the fierce urgency of his embrace as much as the explosion within her. She clung to him, half afraid he'd run, and met his lips with the fire of her own. His tongue found hers, and her knees all but gave way. He held her by the waist, crushing her to him, his hands harsh against the delicate material of her dress. She felt him against her skin like a brand, as if her clothes were no barrier. The fever penetrated her, flaring like embers that had long cooled until Matt's touch fanned them back to brilliant life. To a life more vivid than she'd ever known. Lights seemed to dance in the dim room and music drift in on the wind that rustled through the trees outside. Matt's cologne intoxicated her. His touch sparked unbearably sweet agony. From the moment he took her in his arms, the rest of her world evaporated, and she sank into a whirling vortex of delight.

He slid the knot of her belt and let it fall so that her dress whispered against her, sensuous to his touch. His hands searched her, his kiss claimed her. He tasted her ears, her throat, tracing the throbbing pulses in her neck with his tongue. Kelly arched against him, and the emeralds glittered as she moved.

She opened his shirt and slid it from his arms. It seemed that she couldn't be close enough to him, even pressed against his chest, her fingers roaming restlessly among the hair that curled against her cheek. She felt as if she couldn't breathe, as if she'd been caught under water and couldn't get up.

When Matt kissed her again, he explored her open lips and moved to nip at her earlobes. Kelly felt the molten glow of his touch seep through her, as if she would surely glow from its heat. Her breathing was becoming ragged. Matt's pulse seemed to thunder against her. He slid the dress from her, and then her slip, to lie like a cloud at her feet.

Suddenly he drew back, holding her from him as if trying to consider what he was doing. His eyes were ravaged by the emotions that tore at him. "Kelly, I..."

"Matt," she said firmly, her hands against his chest, her smile wide even as she struggled to breathe. "Shut up."

She surprised an answering smile from him. With one graceful movement, he swept her up into his arms and carried her without effort upstairs to lay her in the big four-poster bed. He finished undressing her with the gentlest of hands until all she wore were her jewels. Then he slipped out of the rest of his own clothes.

Kelly could hardly bear the waiting. He was so beautiful, his strong body lean and fit, his belly flat and his hips narrow. When he lay next to her, she slid her hands around him to his small, tight buttocks and held him tightly against her.

Just as Kelly knew he would, Matt brought her to life, built her passion like the lush movement of a symphony. Slowly, tenderly, his brilliant azure eyes returning time and again to seek the fire in hers, he sought out the exquisitely sensitive skin she had so long hidden away. With those long, graceful fingers he traced her breasts and then took each in hand, his callused hand igniting patterns of fire and exciting her nipples to stiff buds. And then as his hands explored further, from the gentle slope of her belly to the warm strength of her thighs, he bent to taste the breasts his hands had inflamed.

Kelly moaned, eyes closed, hands desperately clutching the muscles of his back as if to stabilize herself. She didn't hear the grandfather clock chime down the hall or feel the cool wind that tugged at her hair and deliciously cooled her damp cheeks and neck. She only felt the fire of Matt's touch, heard his murmurs against her, tasted the bruising headiness of his kisses.

By the time those broad, strong fingers found the moist ache that waited for them, the world had gone scarlet, pulsing, the rhythm reaching Kelly's undulating hips. He brought his mouth down on hers to still the small cries, his tongue duplicating the fiery dance of his fingers. She arched, struggled, pushing and pulling at him, the agony too great to bear.

And then, when she thought she couldn't stand it

anymore, his fingers fled. She arched up to him, tears sparkling in the dark hair that lay tangled on the pillow, eyes wide and liquid with the desire that consumed her. Matt looked into her eyes, the sea-green vivid like gems, his forehead damp and glistening. Kelly wanted to taste it, wanted to devour him until she'd had her fill. Then he entered her, and all that was left was the mesmerizing passion in his eyes, and the shattering light that exploded in her.

She curled around him, pulling him impossibly closer, moving in quickening rhythm with him, rocketing to a brilliant peak she didn't know was possible. She heard his gasping cry that echoed her own, and felt the power of him in her. And when he buried his head against her throat, his chest still heaving, she cradled his beautiful head in her hands and offered him new tears. Her body glowed with a sweetness that took her strength. The wind found her again and cooled her hot, flushed skin. For the moment she could think no further than the bittersweet joy of what she'd just shared. And that was how she fell asleep.

It was not how she woke again. The sun had risen, the morning light filling the room with its tawny warmth. An early morning breeze washed the hot, tangled sheets. Kelly opened her eyes to see the empty bed and hear the shower running.

She should have hopped out of bed and snuck into the bathroom, surprising Matt as he stood lathered and glistening in the shower. She used to do it all the time with Michael, playing the game like hide-and-seek and ending up making love within the delicious curtain of the shower. Instead, she lay where she was, the sheet to her neck, and stared at the ceiling.

The terror had begun to chase her the minute she'd fallen asleep. The cold, sweating walk through a dark night where unnamed specters followed. She wanted so much to tell Matt to wait, that she'd buy a parka or any damn thing she needed to follow him. She wanted to tell him that she had never been so breathtakingly alive as she had been in his arms. But she knew that she couldn't. There was no sense to it, no way to reason her way through it. She just knew that she had to let him go as he'd suggested, and hope she was strong enough to love him when he came back.

"Kelly."

She looked over, startled to see Matt appear in her doorway. He was already dressed.

"Wait," she protested, sitting up. "I'll get dressed and drive you."

"No. I've already called a cab." He walked up and sat on the edge of the bed, his eyes more bittersweet in the morning light. He hadn't understood that when Kelly had run from the voices in her dreams she had to also cower from him. "You stay here. I don't want to have to say good-bye in a crowd."

Kelly tried to smile through the tears his words gave birth to, her hand to his cheek. "Life's going to be kind of boring without you around."

Matt grinned a little and took her hand in his own to kiss it. "If you need me, call. I'll be there."

She nodded. "Me, too." When she looked into his eyes this time, she couldn't look away. The turmoil should have shaken the room. "Till January."

Matt nodded back and then, taking her into his arms as tenderly as if she would break, kissed her. Kelly's arms came up instinctively to that broad back that she so loved, and held him to her again. But only for a moment. The doorbell rang downstairs, and Matt straightened.

"Till January," he said with a smile. "I love you."

Kelly sat very still as he walked away. She sat while he opened the door downstairs and walked out. And when she heard the doors slam and a taxi start down the street, she gave way to tears.

CHAPTER 10

I t was December again.

Kelly hated December with its cold wet wind and dismal skies. Since the leaves had all fallen, she hadn't seen much worth in the scenery. It seemed that she could never get her house warm enough. Work had been slow and boring, the shifts dragging interminably on, and the usual busy work that kept her occupied on slow nights suddenly wasn't all that interesting.

Rich had become a more frequent and understanding suitor, doing his best to counter the effects winter would have on Kelly. Missy organized intricate forays into city and countryside and played a slew of practical jokes to at least keep Kelly distracted. Nothing seemed to cheer her.

December. Why had Michael died in December? He couldn't have waited until a time that wasn't quite so painful. He should have foregone the idea altogether and stuck around another twenty years or so.

Last year Kelly had gone through the month numbly, the effort of just surviving taking all her energy. This year, when she'd thought it would be a little better, it was worse. A vague, pursuing nightmare and the unreasoning terror for Matt's safety completely sapped her tolerance for the festive season. Ever since Matt had left, she'd found herself addicted to news and entertainment reports, waiting fatalistically for some disaster to occur. She hadn't had a decent night's sleep in almost two months, even now that the nightmares were beginning to recede again. And then, her father had called to invite her again to Chicago for the holidays, his voice too stiffly formal. Too many pains to deal with. Still too much pressure from the notoriety of Matt's visit.

The only thing that saved her, as he had known it would, was Matt's distance. Kelly knew that if he were there with his brilliant eyes and gentle hands, the emotions would be more than she could handle.

Two weeks before Christmas, Kelly arrived at work to find the usual slow routine and bored colleagues. She hung up her coat and gloves in her locker, massaging at the reddened tips of her ears and wishing that she could at least get rid of the leaden weight that sat in her stomach.

"Where have you been?" Missy demanded, appearing from the lounge. "I've been trying to get you all day."

"Out." Kelly smiled dryly, knowing that Missy worried like a mother hen this time of year. "I took a walk in Shaw's Garden."

Sitting alone in her silent house, she'd been struck by the idea, as if she could find along those well-trod paths a ghost of warmth left over from the autumn. But the trees were skeletal and cold, the carefully manicured gardens bare. The garden was as lonely as every other place she went.

Kelly followed Missy back into the lounge and settled into a chair. "What's so urgent?" Silly question. Everything was urgent with Missy.

"Rich was just by looking for you," she said, her eyes bright and analyzing.

Kelly wanted to tell her to stop. Missy knew it would be easy for Kelly to rely too much on Rich—on his quiet, gentle support. She kept warning Kelly not to "settle for him."

Kelly usually refrained from answering Missy's innuendos, but today she eyed her friend evenly.

"He asked me to marry him last night."

Missy almost fell off her chair, stiffening with restraint. "What did you tell him?"

Kelly didn't answer immediately. She finished pouring her coffee and stirred in cream and sugar, thinking of how Matt would absently stir at his coffee as he talked. Damn him.

"I told him no." She could hear Missy sigh, and turned on her, anger flashing briefly in sapphire eyes. "On second thought, why shouldn't I marry him?"

Missy never flinched. "Because you don't love him. And because if you married him, not only would it be unfair to him—and you know it. You'd never come back to life."

"You call this coming to life?" Kelly challenged face to face. "Haven't you been hanging around the past two months? I'd have more fun at the Inquisition, Miss."

"You think it's going to be any better if you stay away from him?"

Kelly turned away then to reclaim her seat. "It's getting better already. The press is losing interest, and I'm looking forward to my first night of uninterrupted sleep soon. Now all that's left is the support of my friends." She spit out the last word as if it were a challenge.

Missy stood right up to it. "Your friends aren't going to stand by and watch you throw your life away. You haven't even answered his letters..."

"Letter. Saying that his mother was okay. We've had this discussion before, Missy."

"So you're going to put off dealing with Matt until he appears on your doorstep."

Kelly shrugged, hiding behind the coffee cup as she sipped from it. "Probably."

Missy responded by immediately beaming. Kelly stared at her with undisguised surprise.

"Good!" Missy leaned forward in her chair, arms on knees, her enthusiasm bubbling to the surface. "At least we'll get in our vacation before you'll have to think about it."

Kelly still stared. "Why is that so exciting?"

"Because I didn't want to spoil our two weeks with hand wringing and teeth gnashing. Especially since we'll be going someplace new."

Kelly sat up and took notice at that. "What are you talking about? The reservations are already made. We're going to Keystone."

Missy reached into her pocket and pulled out a letter. Instead of showing it to Kelly, she eyed it herself as if rereading the news it held would spur her on. Her eyes lit up even more brightly. "Oh, why go to Colorado when we can go someplace so much... warmer? Wouldn't you love the chance of an exotic vacation? I mean, what does Keystone have but snow and John Denver? And who's ever met John Denver anyway?"

"He's in Aspen, not Keystone," Kelly corrected automatically. "Missy, what's going on? What exotic vacation?"

Missy grinned broadly, drawing out the suspense, the letter still clutched tightly in her grasp. "Hawaii."

Kelly blanked. "What?"

"Hawaii. Well, Maui, to be exact. God, Kelly, just think of it. Hawaii for Christmas. I'm gonna have to lose weight. I've got this great suit, and where do you get suntan lotion this time of year? A private home, right on the beach! No tourists, no hotels, free room and board..."

"Missy, stop! What are you talking about?"

"Just say yes and make me your grateful slave till my dying day."

Kelly stopped, the light dawning. "Who's the letter from?"

"Say yes and I'll tell you. Just think, Kel, Hawaii. Aloha *hoi* and all that."

"Who?"

"He won't even be there."

"No." Kelly stood and grabbed the letter.

Missy ducked just in time. "Just listen."

"Missy, come on. I'm still trying to get over the last carnival ride."

"He won't be there," Missy repeated emphatically, standing to face Kelly. "His family will be staying there over Christmas, and Matt just couldn't get over the idea that neither of us have a family to spend Christmas with. His family was delighted with the idea. Matt's already made arrangements for us to travel first class, and his mother will meet us at the airport. Matt will still be in Greenland on location." She had to consider that a minute, and responded with an appropriate face. "I sure hope he likes his Christmas white."

"No."

Kelly began to walk out of the lounge, but Missy

caught her by the shoulders and faced her with steady determination. ""Listen to me, Kelly. You're not going to survive if you don't take some chances. There are the big chances like Matt, so maybe that takes a little longer to dig up the guts for. This is a not-so-big chance. A nice vacation with a bunch of nice people. If you turn that down, you might as well crawl back in your house and seal up the door right now, cause if you don't have the guts for that, you won't have the guts for any of it.

"I'll tell you something else," she continued, her eyes earnest. "For some reason, this year I think I'd like to spend my Christmas with someone who enjoys it. And neither of us exactly qualifies. What could it hurt?"

There were so many unnamed emotions that tried to answer, that Kelly couldn't manage. There were too many things she didn't even think she could admit to Missy. Again she fought the tears and won, wondering what it would hurt to fly off to sunny Hawaii instead of battling the old White Christmas blues. It was just that it was Matt's family, the people who had nurtured him and shaped him into the person he was. The person she loved more than she could admit.

"I don't know, Missy," she finally said. "I just don't know. Let's just go to work and forget about it for a while. Maybe I'll be able to think better later."

"Oh, of course. Honey, if you think I can forget it for ten minutes, you're nuts. So if you don't want to talk about it, just don't get upset when you see my pleading, groveling eyes on you."

Kelly's smile was dry. "I'll just pretend you're Gunga Din and slap you." She'd made a move to leave the lounge when she turned back with a new thought. "Why did Matt write you?"

Missy grinned. "'Cause I'm cuter. He's been fantasizing about seeing me in a swimsuit, I know. He also thought that you'd need a little coercing. You know for someone who's only known you for two weeks, he's got a pretty good lead on you."

"If that's your idea of groveling," Kelly retorted, "try again."

Missy shrugged. "When you accept the inevitable, I'll call to finalize the plans." She turned to go, mimicking a hula. "Aloha, Kel."

Kelly threw a book at her.

For the next few days, everyone moved around Kelly as if walking on eggshells. She knew that Missy considered this situation too important to jeopardize by a careless remark, and it was interesting to see her friend strain for the necessary tact.

The decision was driving her into an old-fashioned anxiety attack. She wanted to go, wanted for Missy to be able to get her dream holiday in Hawaii. She wanted to give herself the same thing, complete with the happy, loving family atmosphere she knew existed in Matt's home.

But it was *Matt's* family. That in itself should be enough to make her turn down the offer. It would be like rubbing salt into a fresh wound.

She knew that she couldn't put off the decision any longer when Matt's mother called long distance to rave about the weather and holiday preparations as if talking to one of her own daughters. Kelly wanted more than anything to get to know the person behind that voice.

After hanging up, Kelly sat staring at the empty overcast sky and vacillated. It was only two days until they were supposed to leave. Missy was hypertensive. And Kelly just really wanted to sit in her living room

chair and stare out the window. When she reached for
the phone to give Missy her answer, her hand shook.

IT WAS three o'clock on December sixteenth when the
Air Hawaii jet began to descend for its landing. Maui
swept toward them from beneath a cloud, and the sun
struck its emerald-backed cliffs like a spotlight. Kelly
caught her breath with the sight. After the frigid gray
of St. Louis's winter, the colors seemed brilliant, the
sun softer. Missy spent half a roll of film just capturing
the splendor of white foam breaking against lush
shorelines, and the undulations of an island shaped
like two Hershey kisses that had melted together. The
water was so clear around the island that Kelly could
even see the seabed as they neared.

As they swooped in to land at the small airport,
Missy turned to flash Kelly a triumphant look. "You
look like a kid who just opened the door to the candy
shop."

Kelly refused to look at her, even though she was
grinning. "Oh, shut up."

She recognized Mrs. Hennessy the minute she saw
her. How she wasn't sure, since Matt's mother was
about an inch shorter than she was and probably ten
pounds lighter. Maybe it was the patient way she dealt
with the bright, gamboling young girl next to her.
Kelly imagined that she'd have to have that kind of
imperturbable attitude to put up with Matt, much less
his sudden celebrity.

"You have to be Kelly," the woman sang out with
delight, both arms outstretched in greeting. Kelly felt
perfectly comfortable accepting the warm hug. "Matt's
told me so much about you. I'm glad we could con-

vince you to join us. And Missy!" Another hug was
dispensed, and then she turned to include her daughter. "This is Emily, Matt's sister."

Emily was probably twelve or so, just at the stage
where her looks hadn't quite caught up with her growing. She was too long in some places, too small in others, and contained her excitement awkwardly. She was
already at least a head taller than Kelly and as fair as
Matt was dark.

"Oh, gross!" she gaped. "You guys are white to the
max."

Mrs. Hennessy grinned as she led them through to
baggage. "We've been here three whole days, Em. Give
them time."

"You're, like, a nurse?" Em asked Kelly.

"Exactly like a nurse." Kelly nodded with a grin.
"Only shorter."

Emily, broke up, like, totally, and immediately
took Kelly under her wing to explain the facts of life
as they applied to the islands. By the time they
reached the house, Emily was invited along on Kelly's
and Missy's next ski trip, and Emily vowed that she'd
like to be a nurse like Kelly—only taller. Kelly could
see that Matt's mother had more and more trouble
keeping her secret smiles to herself as the time
sped by.

Matt's house was up the Nāpali coast from the hotels. A simple, oriental-style ranch, it was set on an en-
closed acre that fenced a white beach. Its furnishings
were simple and bright, with a few overstuffed
couches and chairs in primary colors to complement
the rugs and wall hangings that decorated the rooms.
Wind chimes hung everywhere, greeting them with
the never-ending music of the trade winds that
washed through the rooms whose walls were mostly

sliding glass. Kelly walked around silently waiting to be brought back to reality.

Everywhere she looked, she saw the emerald hills give way to verdant mountains in one direction, and the translucent sea in the other. The sea that was the color of Matt's eyes. Kelly couldn't believe it. It was the first time in her life that she'd seen the Pacific Ocean, and yet after knowing Matt for a short time, she'd seen all of its colors and moods reflected in his eyes.

"Well," Mrs. Hennessy said, her gentle fair features wreathed in a smile of anticipation Kelly recognized from knowing her son, "you two only have two weeks to get the tans of your lives. You'd better get started. I'll call you for dinner when Matt's dad and brother get back from golf."

Twenty minutes later Kelly lay on a beach chair waiting for Missy. The sun warmed her limbs, gently soothing away tensions that had threatened so closely only hours before. She decided that she should tell Missy that she'd been right. This had been a good idea. She already felt less harried, less despondent, and knew that she'd found her comfort as much in Matt's family as in the hypnotizing peace of the islands.

"Well, don't you look disgusting."

Kelly looked up to see Missy approach, hands on hips. She wore a stunning magenta string bikini that only Missy could get away with.

"I'll show you disgusting," Kelly retorted. "Go sun-bathe on a different beach, will you? Who did you get to paint that on for you?"

Missy's grin was at once deprecating and pleased. "Some of us like to advertise it, honey, since it doesn't come naturally. And some of us who should have Wide Load painted across our hips can't wear white.

Do you know I really hate you. I've always wanted to wear a suit like that. Too bad Matt can't see you right now. I could call him in East Slobovia if you want."

Kelly appraised her own white wraparound maillot and scowled. It did show some hopefully tempting cleavage, but the high-cut hips just proved that she had none. "Let's just sunbathe."

Considering the time difference, it wasn't that difficult for Kelly to fall asleep, her book open on her stomach. It felt so wonderful and warm, the sea washing rhythmically nearby, the wind ruffling through her hair and cooling the sun. St. Louis and Christmas could almost seem to belong to another lifetime.

"C'mon, kid, time to eat!"

Kelly heard Missy, but she didn't want to pay attention. Maybe no one would mind if she didn't eat tonight. It was just too much effort to get up.

"C'mon, Kelly, we have things to do and people to see!"

"In a while," Kelly mumbled, shifting a little for comfort.

"No. Now."

Kelly sighed, knowing perfectly well that she would expend a lot less energy by just giving in. She stayed still as long as she could, her eyes closed to avoid confrontation as she tried to work up some interest in moving.

Suddenly, something was wrong. She couldn't place it, couldn't put a name to it. Something was out of place. The hairs on the back of her neck bristled, and a chill chased down her spine. It was only a feeling, a visceral reaction with no thought process to define it, and it unnerved her.

Kelly opened her eyes, suddenly afraid to move

and unsure why. The sun lay nestled in a bank of clouds before her, shading the sea that still slid unperturbed to the shore and away again. Behind her, the wind brushed through the trees and clattered through the wind chimes.

Her stomach jolted again. What was it? The air. Something about the air was wrong. She inhaled carefully, identifying the aromas of saltwater, a faint touch of fish and barbecue smoke. Plumeria. And something else. Something she couldn't quite pull from her memory.

"Missy?" She didn't move. Missy had already gone, and Kelly felt even more unsettled. She could feel someone close by her, just beyond her sight.

Oh, God. Pines. She smelled pines where there were none, and suddenly she knew why.

CHAPTER 11

He stood just behind her, smiling. Cool and handsome, he was dressed in a white linen shirt and tan slacks, his feet bare, his hair longer now, ruffled by the wind that found it. He'd grown a mustache and it suited him well. Kelly couldn't speak and could hardly breathe for the shock of pain the sight of him brought her. She'd spent three long months trying to suppress the longing that now leaped in her like a wild thing. The sight of Matt's seawater eyes and little-boy enthusiasm gripped her like a steel band constricting her chest.

He didn't wait for her to greet him. He came over to her and pulled her to her feet, his hands on her arms, his eyes alight.

"You know what?" He grinned a little too brightly. "I forgot how beautiful you were. I missed you, Kelly."

His fingers were like brands against her skin, and she shivered with the thrill of it. She could hardly control her voice. Her eyes looked like saucers.

"I thought you were in...in..."

"Greenland," he said with a nod, not moving to release his grip. "I was. I thought Hawaii would be more fun."

Suddenly Kelly suspected collusion. It would be just like him to plan this little surprise behind her back. She pulled away from him. "Did Missy lie to me? Did she know you'd be here?"

Matt raised his hands in self-defense, his grin broadening. "Missy had no idea," he promised. "In fact, my mother's still in shock. We wrapped up a little early, and I wanted to be back with my family for Christmas. Besides, I wanted an excuse to see you again."

Kelly knew that he'd meant to deliver the last words in a lighthearted way, a tease. The minute he said them, though, his eyes gave him away. The months he'd waited and dreamed, the fear and antici- pation of what he'd find when he got back. Kelly had to look away.

For a moment, they couldn't seem to face each other. It had been two months since Kelly had seen Matt, and yet suddenly it was as if it had been only minutes, and yet torturous years. And where once they'd been so at ease with each other, they now stood at a stiff kind of attention. Kelly felt more uncomfort- able with him than she ever had before.

"You're looking fit," she managed, desperate to find that ease, wishing and afraid that he would touch her again. "The mustache is a nice touch."

She really saw, the closer she looked, how strained the months on location had left him. He looked pale and drawn, the lines around his mouth etched just a little too deeply when he smiled. Just that realization made her afraid, because it made her hurt even more. With all her heart she wanted to hold him against her, stroking his head as he slept, easing the pressure and isolation she saw. She wanted to make the difference that would help him survive the demands the world put on him. And yet, for the first time since they'd met, she couldn't seem to reach him. It was as if the torture of their time apart had constructed an unseen barrier between them.

"A compromise," Matt said with a grin, fingering the soft brown mustache. "The PR department thought the public liked me better hairy."

It was Kelly's turn to consider. "Oh, I don't know. I think you could get away with just about anything."

They stood for a moment in pressing silence. "Hey, Kelly," he offered, putting his hands out to her. "How about a walk on the beach?"

"No...uh, I think dinner's just about ready," she said, demurring awkwardly. "You could use some meat on those bones."

He nodded perfunctorily. "Then we'll sit and talk. Tell me about St. Louis."

He sat in Missy's chair and waited for Kelly to follow. Slowly she sat back down.

"Not much to tell." She felt as uptight as if she were on a first date. "How've you been?"

His eyes searched hers as if looking for something her words lacked.

"Oh, mostly cold and wet. The movie's not going to be Oscar material. Has the limelight dimmed a little in your neck of the woods?"

Kelly nodded, desperately trying to quell the urge to run to him. "Yeah. They show up from time to time just to make sure you haven't snuck back into town on the red-eye. It's still disconcerting to see myself on the news when they catch me."

"The news?" he retorted instinctively. "You don't watch..."

Even before he could finish the sentence, his half grin died. His eyes clouded with the pain of understanding what Kelly had been through because of him.

Kelly looked away again, picking up her book and closing it with trembling hands. "Well," she finally managed, "I'd better get dressed."

Matt stood with her, but didn't move for the house. Kelly found herself waiting before him. His eyes had darkened, and he reached out again to take hold of her arms gently, almost hesitantly. "This isn't right, Kelly. We're acting like we've never met before." He scowled playfully, trying to lighten the tone of his suddenly serious voice. "You haven't been reading the *Enquirer* again have you?"

She had to grin at that, relaxing a little. "No, Matt —" she shook her head, trying to keep the tone light "—I'm just having a little trouble with your being here." A lot of trouble, she thought with a shaky breath. "You said January, and I counted on that. I'm much more susceptible to surprises in December. And my social skills are totally lacking. That's why Missy and I usually go to Colorado. If I'm surly to anyone, at least it's usually to somebody I don't know."

Matt saw the pain in Kelly's eyes and drew her gently to him before she could protest. "It was kind of thoughtless of me, wasn't it? Like you said, sometimes I have the sensitivity of a jackhammer."

"Comes from being such a patient person," Kelly murmured.

Matt bent his head over hers, his hand once again affectionately stroking her hair. "I'm very patient. Also understanding. I'll tell you what. I have a little pent-up surliness I could get rid of. We'll just be nasty to each other, and then we won't have to bother insulting anyone else."

Kelly eased into the comfort of his arms and allowed herself the luxury of encircling him with her own. The heady peace made her pause before answering, and Matt kept the silence. The world suddenly slipped comfortably back into place, and Kelly didn't want to disturb it She felt as if she'd just walked back into her home after a long time away. She felt Matt's stillness and knew that he felt it, too.

"Sounds like a good idea to me," she finally answered him. "I like your mom too much to hurt her feelings."

"I thought you two would hit it off," he said enthusiastically. "She thinks you're the most stable woman I've met in years."

"I am."

"You are, huh?" he retorted even more heartily, holding her back at arm's length. "In that case, you'll be the one to go on my Kauai trek this year."

"Your what?"

"For the past three years I've made it to Christmas from location, and I've been so nasty that Mom's thrown me out for two or three days before she even let me unpack. This year, you can come with me. We'll both be angels by Christmas Eve."

He took her by the hand and turned for the house. Kelly stopped him.

"Oh, Matt, I don't think so," she protested anxiously.

"Why not?" he retorted, his whole demeanor so like those first days she'd known him. "I doubt sincerely that the press will be along."

"Please, Matt," she begged, tears burning her eyes again. "Don't push. I can't tell you how hard the past two months have been on me. It took all the courage I had just to come meet your family."

She couldn't yet tell him how fiercely she loved him, how just the sight of him made her want to sing and cry with relief. But the memory of her torment must have shown in her eyes. Matt turned back to her, taking her by the arms, the pale depths of his eyes brimming with love.

"See?" he challenged gently. "I said you had courage. The rest will come."

She tried her best to smile even as her chest caught fire. "You are one great optimist, aren't you?"

He smiled back, his eyes never wavering. "That's the only way to be, sweet Kelly. The only way."

He stood very still, his eyes searching hers, his grip still tight. She was held there by his eyes, barely breathing, her heart echoing in her ears. The current jumped between them then—a hot, living thing, and Kelly realized how much sweeter the wind felt, how the ocean pulsated like the rush of blood through her arteries.

Matt drew her to him, his arms crushing the breath from her. His mouth, at once gentle and possessive, sweeter than anything Kelly had known, found hers and forced it open. She felt his breath on her neck, the heady warmth of his arms, and closed her eyes to it. At once in the brief moment he held her she came alive again, each nerve tingling. The fire at her core caught and flared, a thrilling pain that made her gasp.

Matt lifted his head without easing his grasp. His eyes had darkened again and he was a little out of breath. "Ever since I left St. Louis, I've been thinking how you felt in my arms. It's even better than I remembered."

"Then I wasn't the only one," she retorted with a shaky half grin. "I was always looking around for the shorted-out wire I kept touching."

His smile was hers alone. "Sometimes I think we should have met at some other time or place." He loosened his grip a little, his smile becoming enigmatic. "And sometimes I have the disturbing feeling that maybe we have."

Kelly tried to match the flippancy of his smile and with one of her own. "If it weren't for our ghosts, and our jobs, and the kind of people we are, we might have been Gable and Lombard."

"Napoleon and Josephine."

"More like Gary Grant and Minnie Pearl," she retorted, still trying her best to play the game, wanting nothing more than to remain within his life-giving embrace where the day seemed so much kinder, knowing all the while what the cost would be. Her demons were already beginning to eat at her.

Matt's smile broadened as he kissed her forehead. "You've got it backward," he said. "I'd say it's more like Grace Kelly and Red Buttons."

"Well, c'mon, Red," she said, grinning, easing away and wondering if she would be able to withstand the easing of their discomfort. "Let's go eat."

Matt took her hand, his lively smile more familiar. "Right behind ya, Grace."

That night, for the first time in two weeks, Kelly awakened from a sound sleep, her heart racing and her palms slippery with sweat. Still the dream refused to surface. She felt only the fear and an overwhelming sense of loss. She lay for a long time staring at the ceiling. Listening to the soothing ocean, she tried to will the ghosts away.

Her tension didn't ease appreciably over the next

few days, but Kelly found herself better able to deal with it. Matt was carefully noncommittal, keeping his promise not to pressure her, and for all appearances happy with it. Kelly found herself enjoying her time with him, content to leave the important discussions for another day. She didn't want to tamper with what was shaping up to be the happiest two weeks she could remember.

One of the reasons Kelly enjoyed her surprise vacation so much was the care and camaraderie of Matt's family. They took Kelly and Missy into the family without reservation and made them feel right at home. Kelly found that she envied Matt the family he took for granted. His mother was warm, bright and open, with arms that could embrace the world. His father, John, was a quiet man with a slow smile and a dry wit who gave his loyalty unfailingly once it was earned. At six feet, he was dwarfed by the son who'd made famous his weathered good looks. It was only when Kelly saw him look at his tiny wife that she understood how he could be the romantic Matt painted him to be. He absolutely melted in the woman's presence.

Emily was a bright, eager child who consumed life in huge, happy gulps. Her oldest brother was the light of her life, and she made no bones about it, constantly pestering him and playing adolescent pranks on him.

Matt's younger brother Tim was about Kelly's age, another handsome brunette with his mother's eyes, who spent a lot of time telling a wide-eyed Missy about the computers he'd designed back in California.

It wasn't until she'd been there four days that Kelly recognized the peace she felt with these people. They were the family she and Missy had been searching for all these years. There was no pain here, no rejection, no guilt. For the first time since she was eighteen, Kelly knew the feeling of security and peace.

It was Missy who informed her, the morning she caught Kelly singing, that Kelly's chronic December depression had disappeared like a damp mist. When Kelly thought about it, she realized that she hadn't felt like singing since Michael had died.

"Does this mean you're going to move in with Matt's family?" Missy demanded mischievously.

Kelly shook her head as she watched Matt work on the bougainvillea that lined his lawn. Just the sight of him sent both pain and joy racing through her. "Too much of a commute."

"For a family like this," Missy retorted more seriously than she'd intended, "I'd sell out and move."

It took Kelly a long time to answer, her eyes out on the lawn. "I'm just not so sure that's an option."

Missy, standing across the room, made a distinct face of disgust and set her hands emphatically on her hips. "For God's sake, girl, when are you gonna stop mooning over that man and do something about it? You've had four whole days, and so far you two act like blind dates at a high school dance."

Kelly turned on her friend. "And I'm still having nightmares from just being around him. What do you think would happen if I let myself really go?" Missy's eyes widened a little at the emotion in Kelly's voice, but she didn't move. It was the first time Kelly had allowed herself even this much. "You weren't the one held down on a table, Missy. You weren't the one spending your overtime money on a psychologist eight months ago so you could try to stop blaming yourself for at least one of the deaths in your life."

Missy stood her ground, eyes soft with the shared

memory of Kelly's pain. "And you think that if you love Matt, he'll die too?"

Kelly glared for a moment, posture still rigid. Then she seemed to slump. "No," she admitted with a small shake of her head. "I don't think that's it. I'm just afraid of loving him too much and losing him. I'm afraid it would break me." Kelly walked over and sat on the bed, her hands rubbing the tops of her knees as if the movement brought comfort. "Not necessarily rational, I know. But people aren't always rational. If they were, Daddy wouldn't still be blaming me for Mom's death, and I wouldn't blame myself for Michael's. I'm just not sure I'm strong enough, anymore, for anything more intense than a quiet life with somebody like Rich." When she looked up at Missy this time, her eyes were brimming with the tears Matt had brought back. "Somebody who doesn't scare me so much."

Kelly woke again that night sweating and shaking. It was almost two in the morning. The house was dark, with only the rhythmic pulse of the ocean to keep her company. She knew it would be a while before she could get back to sleep, so she put on a robe and slipped out onto the patio to enjoy a bit of romantic Hawaiian night air.

Outside, a crescent moon skirted the tops of gently swaying palm trees. Stars dusted the sky and reflected on the moving water where the breakers gleamed like iridescent slashes across the sea. The sights and sounds soothed her. The strange pull of a forgotten dream eased, and the stumbling staccato of her heartbeat slowed.

"I thought I heard someone else up."

Kelly looked up to see Matt, sleep tousled and smiling. Somehow it seemed appropriate for him to

be there. In the anonymity of night, their barriers fell
away and they were friends again.

"Have a seat," she offered, moving to give him
space on her lawn chair. "What are you doing up so
late?"

He shrugged, sitting. "I think I'm still on Greenland time. I've been having trouble getting back into
routine. You?"

"I woke up."

"Nightmare?"

She shrugged back. "Either that or hot flashes. Not
so bad tonight, though."

Matt's eyes gleamed softly in the small light
thrown from the house. "You should always look like
this, Kelly. It suits you."

"What, bloodshot and bleary eyed?" She grinned,
his attention somehow not so threatening beyond the
boundaries of daylight. "I look like the first scene in
Bride of Frankenstein."

He grinned, reaching out to touch the hair that
tumbled about her shoulders. "No wonder the big ga-
loot fell for her."

Kelly savored the thrill of his touch. "You sure have
a way with compliments."

Matt's hand stayed on her shoulder, his eyes
moving to her own. She could see his ease, his open-
ness in the mask of night, and with it his arousal.
Without taking his eyes from her, he let his hand trail
along her arm. He traced her fingers with gentle
strokes and then sought the belt of her robe. Kelly felt
the warning tingle of his aura, knew that he was about
to come too close. The nightmare seemed to have become lost, though. Kelly couldn't seem to locate her
fear in this frail, magical light and found herself
smiling lazily at him.

"Just what do you think you're doing?"

She realized that her voice was becoming husky and it unaccountably amused her. This wasn't like her at all. Maybe she could blame it on the seductive Hawaiian moon or the bewitching hour of the night. Or on Matt. He should have at least worn a shirt when he came out. The light threw his chest into an odd kind of relief that was making her ache to reach out and explore it.

Matt searched her eyes for her meaning, and when he found it, smiled back, the light in his own eyes sending a greater thrill through her than his touch. Kelly could see that he was just as surprised as she at the unexpected turn of events, a gentle, wry glimmer caught his eye. "I think I'm going to make love to you. That all right with you?"

He leaned forward, his one hand untying the knot on her robe and letting it fall away. By the time his bent head blocked out the light, Kelly's eyes were closed. She slid her hand up to the back of his head and held him to her. She opened her lips in invitation and slid her tongue along his to taste the sweetness of his mouth. It seemed as if she hadn't breathed for a very long while by the time she was able to open her eyes again.

"Yes," she said, standing to reach out her hand. "It's all right."

It was so odd. Even as she led him back into her bedroom, she realized that she wasn't afraid. She wasn't thinking about what would happen tomorrow, because in the protection of the night, there didn't have to be a tomorrow. In the soft half-light when anything could be magic, nothing mattered but that moment. They were, for that night, lovers, and no one could ever take that from them.

Matt rarely took his eyes from Kelly's, almost as if he couldn't bear to leave her for an instant. Kelly accepted his touch, the torture of his familiar exploration, and met his gentle gaze, sure she would drown in the depths of his eyes. He slipped the soft velour robe from her shoulders, taking her into the protection of his embrace. She reached up then to stroke his chest. Even the touch of him shocked her, the flow of energy that seemed to leap to her fingertips as they traveled over the delicious hair-roughened contours of his skin. She traced his lean muscles, memorizing them, and circled his satiny nipples to stiffness with her thumbs. Then she followed the path of his ribs around to search the spare line of his back, discovering, learning. He had a scar beneath his left arm, a triangular elasticity that Kelly studied as if capturing a part of Matt for her own. She might never again have the courage to hold anyone so beautiful, so masculine. She wanted to take away with her the memory of him to sustain her.

Matt kissed her, gently exploring soft recesses and tracing her lips, nourishing her with his delight. He moved to her cheeks, her eyes, her hair, nuzzling into it where it tumbled over her neck.

"Your hair smells like sunlight," he whispered.

"Yours smells like soap," Kelly whispered back with a tremulous smile as his lips found her sensitive throat.

"Not very romantic," he mumbled, his attention on the straps of her sheer gown. She wondered if he knew that she'd chosen the color to bring out the blue in her eyes.

"You don't know what turns me on."

She wanted to laugh, to sigh or sing with the bubbling joy Matt radiated like a sensuous aroma. The power of his satisfaction made her want to live forever.

Matt's lips found her breasts and devoured them, leaving a tantalizing moistness that tingled in the night breeze. "I'm trying to find out," he finally muttered.

He cupped a breast in his hand and took the nipple gently in his teeth teasing it to delicious hardness. His used his other hand to discover the satiny skin of her thigh, progressing upward at a maddeningly slow pace. Kelly arched against him, unable to remain still, the fire he'd ignited in her threatening to consume her. When she reached around his waist to pull him against her, to feel the lean strength of his body against hers, she knew that he was just as aroused as she. She deliberately slid his pants over his hips, letting him know without words how desperate she was.

Matt lifted his head, his eyes finding hers and smiling—smiling as if he'd just come home. She led him to her. Then, as she feasted on his eyes she welcomed him with her deep-throated sigh, her hands against the hard lines of his buttocks as she pulled him even deeper. She lifted to him, arching in rhythm, beginning to soar free of the earth, the blue of his eyes the endless open sky. They moved upward together, melding closer and closer until Kelly almost felt that they were one, spiraling into the vastness of the night until she couldn't contain the sweet, hot joy.

Matt enfolded her completely to him, his mouth covering her gasping relief. And then slowly, the night cooled. Kelly's heart slowed and her breathing eased. When she opened her eyes, she saw that Matt glistened with perspiration. He moved just enough to ease his weight and lay for a long time just stroking her hair. Kelly never imagined that she could feel such peace. She didn't want to ever move.

"You're going to fall off the bed," she said quietly to him.

He didn't open his eyes. "I have plenty of room."

Kelly was beginning to shiver as the night breeze found her through the window. "Aren't you just a little chilly?"

Matt lifted a hand and drew it along the ridge of her shoulder until goose bumps covered her chest.

"Sadist," she said with a shiver, huddling closer.

He shifted his weight a little and pulled out the covers over them both, and then he cradled Kelly in his arms.

"How's that?"

"Wonderful." For at least a few more moments, she could feel as if nothing would ever hurt her again, as if Matt would always be there to make her smile.

"Hey," Matt spoke up suddenly, "when are we going to Kauai? Mom hinted again today that as of yet I lack a civil tongue."

"You don't need one. You've got great hands."

He punched her playfully. "That would severely limit my repertoire."

"You're right," she said, giggling. "It's not exactly the best way to try and rent a car."

"So when are we going?"

"I don't want to go to Kauai," she objected, thinking absently how delicious Matt's chest felt against her breast. "I haven't even seen Maui yet."

Kelly's words set off a reaction in Matt. Suddenly he sat up, his eyes alight. He looked down for the watch he'd taken off.

"What time is it?"

"About two-thirty. Why?"

He looked at her, a grin spreading into excitement. She hadn't seen that look since she'd found the hansom cab outside her door.

"You want to see Maui?" he demanded. "Get dressed. And packed. We can be up Haleakala by sunrise."

"What?"

Matt got to his feet, pulling Kelly with him. "It's something not to be missed. After we go there, we'll head up the north coast road and spend a couple of days in Hana."

"Matt..."

"C'mon," he urged, pushing her toward the house. "If you don't hurry, we'll miss it."

By the time she woke Missy to tell her what was going on, Kelly had actually begun to anticipate the spur-of-the-moment trip. The more she hung around Matt, the more she realized how much she enjoyed doing things on a whim. He was the first person to really give her the chance.

That didn't take away the dread, though. She thought of Michael a moment. She'd never known such pain with him, such a maelstrom of sensation and emotion. His love for her had been a peaceful, healing thing that had comforted her. And she had almost not survived his loss.

She hadn't exaggerated to Missy about her fear of losing Matt. It would be like losing life itself—a life that was becoming more and more vital as the days passed. Her head told her to get away, back to the safe and undemanding friendship Rich offered, and not to keep trying for more than she had a right to hope for. But her heart was already walking out the door to watch the sunrise with a madman.

She stood alone in the silence of her room for a

few long minutes, her eyes on the tortured face she saw reflected in the mirror. Then with a definite straightening of her shoulders, she picked up the overnight bag Missy had helped her pack and walked from the room. The gentle, rushing sounds of the ocean followed her.

CHAPTER 12

Matt set off on the pre-dawn jaunt in what Kelly considered to be terminally bright humor. He assured her that in his line of work it wasn't at all unusual for him to be up at ungodly hours of the morning. Kelly assured him right back that if God had wanted her to get up before the sun, He would have had her come equipped with a little miner's lamp in the middle of her forehead. All she could think of was that if she hadn't talked Matt out of visiting Kauai, she could have been back in bed asleep.

Kelly sensed rather than saw most of the climb up Haleakala's dormant crater. All she could see in the path of the headlights was a narrow gravel road that continually turned to the left, with no visible shoulder. Matt supplied statistics and local history as they went along, his enthusiasm infectious enough to keep Kelly awake.

The sky began to lighten as they neared the top, and Kelly was able to first see the attraction of the place and the extent of the climb they'd just made in the car. The road they followed wound around the perimeter of the volcano. From any point there was a dramatic mile-long drop to the valley floor. Kelly had never seen anything so beautiful. It was as if they were in a different world than the one they'd just left. Matt pointed out Mauna Loa where it rose like a sleeping giant from the distant sea and glowered beneath a cloud cover. With the sun's approach, the sea beneath glowed like a brightening pearl.

"Matt, this is incredible," she breathed, trying to see everything at once.

"This is just the overture," he said with a grin.

He was right. They parked by the observation house and walked along the rim of the great crater to a high point and sat huddled against the sharp wind that raked across the wild desolation that was the top of Haleakala. This must be what a moonscape is like, Kelly thought, alien and barren. The undulations of the landscape born of violence and time.

She found herself shivering, as much from the sight as from the wind that continually knifed through the light-weight green jumpsuit she wore. Matt saw her and put an arm around her, drawing her close and sharing her silence. Why is it, she thought, his warmth suffusing her, that I feel as if we were the first people to ever see this sight? Why is it that after sharing it with Matt I don't want to share it with anyone else?

"Watch," Matt whispered, his voice sounding as awed as Kelly's thoughts.

At the horizon the clouds built, climbing over the rim of the crater with majestic beauty, the colors of seashells. The blue of the sky brightened, mirroring the clouds' hues and illuminating the wild grandeur of the landscape that stretched away from their feet. She began to see that it wasn't just the gray of old lava, but also russets, reds, and mauves, all muted and changing.

Then the sun burst over the edge, and the world was transformed. Kelly knew she gaped, moving unconsciously closer to Matt as she faced the primitive splendor of the sight. The sun drenched the clouds and landscape with its fire, tinting everything before it blood red. As they watched, it brought the world to life in a matter of minutes.

Kelly and Matt remained where they were long after the sun had crested the volcano's side. The daylight brought back the colors, and Kelly could see that paths snaked across the crater top, but she thought the place would still never belong to earth.

"What do you think?" Matt finally asked.

Kelly shook her head slowly, at a loss for appropriate words. She could feel Matt's eyes on her with companionable warmth. Turning on him, she grinned mischievously. "It was almost worth getting up at two in the morning for."

He chuckled. "Just for that, I won't let you hike across the crater before we head back."

"You're damn right you won't," she retorted emphatically.

Still grinning, he drew himself up to an indignant pose. "Do you mean that you wouldn't follow me out there?"

"I do."

"You wouldn't follow Matt Hennessy if he asked you to go across that crater with him?"

"Him either."

An eyebrow raised. "I could ask the next woman I see to go with me and she wouldn't so much as hesitate."

Kelly was having trouble keeping a straight face. "Would you like me to pack you two a picnic lunch?"

"She would follow me anywhere!"

Kelly tilted her head in consideration. "Does that mean I have to pack dinner, too?"

Matt broke first, his hearty laughter echoing away across the stillness of the volcano. Behind them, Kelly could hear a car pull into the parking lot.

"You're incorrigible," he accused, pulling her close again.

"I could say the same about you," she retorted with a chuckle. "Probably our most admirable quality."

"Mine, anyway," he corrected. "I'd expect better of you, though."

"I'm just doing you a favor," she objected. "Being rejected can be very good for the artistic soul."

"Is that why I find you so irresistible?" His voice was light. Kelly's chest tightened with the words.

"Your mother and I," she retorted, watching the clouds and soaking in his touch, "the only two people who tell you 'no.'"

Matt looked over at her then, and suddenly his eyes weren't so mischievous. "Do me a favor," he said, his voice soft. "Don't change."

"Isn't that a song cue?"

Kelly wasn't sure she had the nerve to face what could be in his eyes. The time was past when half-hoped impossibilities could seem within reach; when it appeared natural to express the true depth of what they felt for each other. There was no moon now to shade them from the consequences of their actions.

"I mean it, Kelly. Every time I see you it's like a breath of fresh air." He took her hand then and with it demanded her attention. "You're just about the only person other than my family who doesn't either faint dead away or see me as a dollar sign just because I'm a marketing phenomenon."

"And all this time I thought it was because of your eyes," she said gently.

For a moment the light in his eyes was poignant, then his smile brightened. "You're good for me, Kelly."

She tried to grin. "I know."

"Excuse me." Startled by the interruption, the two of them turned. Three tourists, a fairly middle-aged couple and their slack-jawed near-catatonic daughter stood behind them. The mother appeared to be the spokesperson.

"Aren't you Matt Hennessy?"

For the first time since Kelly had known him, Matt failed to slip into character on cue. "No," he said, grinning ruefully without missing a beat. "I wish I were. Then I'd be driving a Porsche instead of a used Jeep."

The three looked totally nonplussed. Again the older woman spoke. "No," she agreed tentatively, eyeing Matt carefully. "I guess you're not. At first glance you sure look like him, though."

"Oh, no," Kelly disagreed, backing away to eye Matt herself. "Matt Hennessy's much more handsome. His eyes are deeper, more soulful, you know? And he's taller. And his chin's more solid."

The woman began to look uncomfortable. "I guess you're right. I'm sorry."

"C'mon," Matt said to Kelly as he helped her to her feet. "Let's go get some breakfast. All this flattery's making me light-headed."

"Just a minute." Kelly hesitated, her eyes wicked. She turned to the family just as they were about to walk on. "Excuse me, do you see those paths out there, across the crater?"

The three turned to look and then turned back to Kelly. Matt was becoming suspicious.

"I just wanted to ask if you'd like to walk across those paths with this man—"

"Kelly," Matt warned blackly.

"You see he told me—" She never got the chance to finish. Matt bodily pulled her away. The three people were beginning to look more than uncomfortable.

"Don't mind her—" Matt placated them even as he was dragging Kelly toward the parking lot "—her therapist says that she won't be doing things like this much longer." He flashed a dazzling smile and turned back on Kelly with a playful scowl. "I was right about you. You are a troublemaker."

Kelly yawned all the way to get coffee then afterward back along the north coast road. She was having serious trouble keeping her eyes open, even with the wind whipping in through the open window.

"Lombard would never fall asleep on Gable," Matt finally accused when she'd yawned the fifth time in as many minutes.

"Yeah, I know. Nobody but me'd fall asleep on Matt Hennessy. Well, this Lombard didn't even get to sleep until midnight last night."

He seemed astonished. "You only got two hours of sleep?"

"Well I hadn't anticipated taking off on a road trip, did I?"

Matt grinned out at the road. "You didn't say no when I asked," he said, gloating. "That's because I know the key to making you say 'yes.'"

A bubble of tension rose in her chest. Silly, useless anticipation. "Oh, yeah? What's that?"

"Romance. You're a sucker for it."

The bubble fell. "Dawn patrol is not my idea of romance," she said with a grimace. "Besides, you're wrong."

"Oh?"

She nodded, avoiding his gaze. To their left, the sun winked off the ocean. "It's that little-boy anticipation of yours when you're waiting for me to find the surprise."

Again Matt looked over, but this time said nothing. When Kelly turned to meet his eyes, she saw the smile in them and was caught again by that fledgling flush of anticipation. An unnamed tension was beginning to build between them, as much from what they didn't say as from what they said.

"I've got an idea." His eyes were back on the road. "You need something to keep you awake long enough to enjoy more of my incomparable charm. How about a visit to my favorite swimming hole?"

"I'd love to," Kelly agreed with only minimal hesitation.

Silence returned, and Kelly found herself easily drawn back to the passing scenery. The narrow road they followed snaked in and out along the winding coastline of north Maui where population was sparsely divided among isolated villages out on tiny peninsulas. The road seemed to cling to the sides of lush cliffs that dropped down straight to the sea. Kelly saw plants she'd managed to kill at home growing here to spectacular heights and sizes: schefflera, ferns of a hundred kinds, philodendron—flowers that tumbled like bright waterfalls through the dense jungle growth. Kelly felt sorry about all the development that had already reached the other side of the island.

Suddenly Matt stopped the car. They were sitting in the middle of the narrow, pitted road, nowhere near civilization. She stared over at Matt in surprise, but he just ignored her until he got the Jeep carefully off the road and onto a rather narrow ledge. Switching off the engine he turned to her, his eyes bright with the anticipation she'd earlier described to him.

"Ready?"

"For what?"

His grin broadened smugly. "Swimming."

Kelly took a moment to peer across to their left. There the undergrowth stopped just beyond the Jeep's fender quite a few feet above the rush of the surf. The shoulder to the right was a solid rock ledge.

She turned back to Matt. "I don't high dive."

"You don't have to—" he smiled broadly "—c'mon."

What Matt had discovered was a path that wound precariously down the side of a rather sudden cliff to a small sandy cove that lay hidden below. It took them fifteen minutes to descend, but Kelly decided in the end that the effort was worthwhile. Hidden back underneath an overhang of rock and trailing tropical foliage, the ocean had carved out a small horseshoe bay of crystal azure water and white sand. It was a quiet, personal place where only bird song intruded.

"You've done it again," Kelly had to admit with an awed shake of the head. Picking up her overnight bag, she backtracked away beyond Matt's field of vision and prepared to change. That was when she realized that Missy had sabotaged her bag. There, carefully folded on top of her towel where she'd packed her white suit, lay the bits of bright cloth Missy called a swimsuit. Obviously Missy's idea of a subtle move. Kelly sighed, holding the suit by its strings. Missy had won this round, and there wasn't anything Kelly could do about it. She would have to wear it, and she wasn't at all sure it would stay on.

When she stepped out onto the beach, she immediately held up a warning hand before a wide-eyed Matt could say a word.

"It's Missy's fault," she said, feeling terribly exposed. "So if you don't mind, no wisecracks. I feel naked enough as it is."

Matt, standing waist deep in the water and looking for all the world like a sea god, smiled. "I was just going to say that color suits you."

Kelly looked down with an uncomfortable grimace. "I didn't think there was enough of it to tell."

When she slid into the water a few minutes later, she found it warm and soothing. She spent a long time swimming, then floating, then swimming again, her strokes deliberately measured. Matt swam alongside, as much at peace with the silence as Kelly. It was as if once again they were the only two people in the world, and Kelly would have given anything for it to stay that way. Every once in a while she took a peek at Matt's face as he floated near her. She felt almost as if she were absorbing the sight of him to save forever, like she would save the sun for the winter days ahead. Taunting herself with him, an alcoholic always wanting just one more drink.

Just beyond Matt, a bright-winged bird skimmed the water to nest in a nearby tree and chatter at them. The morning brightened, and Matt and Kelly floated side by side, desultorily speaking to the clouds.

"God, I could get used to this." Matt sighed, his eyes closed.

"I thought you were," Kelly teased, her eyes closed as well. Her hair drifted gently about her in the water, and the sun was a red warmth against her skin.

"I have to get back to work the same time you do," he protested lightly.

"Got a new film?"

"No. Publicity for the one I just finished."

She squinted over at him. "You poor thing. You have to get all dressed up in a tux and go on television. Why, that's absolutely inhuman."

He splashed her. "Just for that, I'm cutting St. Louis from my tour schedule."

"No you won't," she retorted brightly, splashing back. "You wouldn't miss the chance to throw my life back into chaos, and you know it."

Matt got to his feet and pushed his hair back from his forehead. Kelly looked over at him, amazed again at the colors that reflected in his eyes.

He looked delighted. "I have to admit that I haven't had that much fun on any other publicity tour. The last visit would be hard to top, though. Rich already knows who I am."

Kelly grinned up at a plane that connected the clouds with white vapor trails. "He liked you better as an import-export salesman. Something about that natural ability to improvise."

"You are asking for trouble, lady," Matt threatened, approaching.

Kelly waved his threats away. "You can't scare me, pal. I'll just tell the press I'm pregnant."

He still approached, crouching to appear more threatening. "And I'll tell Sister Agatha."

"That's all right. I'll tell her it's Rich's. He wants to marry me anyway."

That brought him to a dead stop. "You're kidding."

Kelly deliberately closed her eyes again. "He asked me last week."

The bubble of tension was beginning to build again. It was all she could do to remain still.

"You told him no, didn't you?"

She still refused to look over. "What do you think I said?"

She couldn't explain why she was playing this silly game except for the fear that once again rose in her chest.

"You won't marry Rich," Matt scoffed. "You'd die of boredom."

"What should I do instead?" she retorted with careful nonchalance, his nearness beginning to crowd her, her skin bristling as if charged. "Wait for another movie star to jump into my car?"

"Yes," he said, nodding, a curiously bland smile lighting his eyes as he moved even closer. "You like surprises!"

Without warning, he lunged. Before Kelly could react, he tackled her around the waist and the two of them ended up under water. They broke surface together.

"Leave me alone!" Kelly sputtered, unable to keep from laughing.

Matt came after her again, and she ran, splashing through the water. The sounds echoed around the cove and started a few birds from the trees. She had too little on, and the feel of Matt's hair-coarsened skin against hers was too delicious.

"Get away from me!"

"C'mon, Kelly. Tell me you won't marry him."

"I'm not telling you anything!" she shrieked, splashing at him to keep him away.

He just kept grinning, his eyes narrowing on her. "Of course you will," he retorted, his voice husky, his teeth gleaming against his tan. "You'll tell me everything I want to know!"

He made another grab for her and pulled them back into the water. This time when Kelly came up for air, Matt caught her by the arms, and her heart leaped. The current jumped between them, hot and intoxicating. Searing through to her belly, it lay there coiled and tense. She knew she wasn't going to run much longer.

"Matt, stop it. This suit's too fragile," she laughed, trying to pull from the lightning his grasp was unleashing. "It's going to fall off if you don't stop."

"I thought that was the whole idea," he said grinning wolfishly, pulling her against him. "I'd hate for Missy to think she packed that suit for nothing."

Somehow Kelly found the strength to duck away from his hold. "Well, she did!"

Matt ran after her and easily caught her by the arm. "I'm not letting you go until you tell me you won't marry him."

Kelly laughed, breathless. "Just for that, I will marry him!"

Matt pulled her to him. She couldn't move, couldn't breathe at all. The lightning jolted her again, stabbing at her chest and flaring along her limbs. She found herself moving against the curves of Matt's body, instinctively seeking his heat.

"You're going to make me do something rash," he threatened, breathing as hard as Kelly, his eyes melting with arousal. Kelly made the mistake of looking up at them and found that she couldn't look away. The power of his gaze made her nipples strain against the soft material that held them.

"What are you going to do?" she countered, her voice barely audible. "Kidnap me again?"

Matt nodded slowly, smiling, his eyes never leaving hers. "If necessary."

His hands had begun to massage her shoulders.

Kelly almost looked down to see whether she was melting with the heat of his touch.

"I'd hate to see you make a big mistake like that."

She could hardly talk now for the thrilling pain of his touch. She wanted to rub like a cat against his chest, to watch her hands discover the lines of his belly. "What if I've already made up my mind?"

He bent closer, his breath on her cheek. "I'd have to convince you."

When she answered, Kelly hardly recognized the sound of her own voice. She couldn't seem to look away from his eyes, the soft lines of his lips. "Try it."

The world waited on, the sea's pulse punctuating the electric silence. Matt held her, his face just above hers, his eyes seething. The water glistened like gems against his dark hair and tanned skin. A small breeze skittered across the water and chilled the flesh his touch had heated. Kelly's head was back, her eyes up to Matt's, her heart outpacing the sea.

Slowly, deliberately, he bent and gathered her to him. Kelly brought her arms up to circle his neck, the taut muscles cool against her hot fingers. She stood almost chest deep in the water, on her toes to reach up to him, her eyes fixed on his. When he kissed her, she met him with open lips, more hungry if possible than he. When he pulled her even closer with a hand to the back of her neck, she arched against him. The feel of him, rigid against her, drew her hands to his chest. Again, exquisitely, the dormant fire swept through her, fueled by his ravenous touch.

She felt him untie the strings of her suit. The thought briefly crossed her mind that she should stop him because someone would see. But she couldn't. His fingers were too intoxicating. The top and then the bottoms slid off into the water and drifted away. Matt bent to taste the saltiness on her throat, drinking her excitement like nourishment. The scent of him surrounded her, that cool, rich aroma of the mountains. Spiced with the tang of salt, it seemed the most delicious elixir Kelly had ever known.

She clung to him, desperate from the months he'd been away and for the future she so feared. She loved him more than she had loved anyone else. In the sunlight she had nowhere to hide her love, and it fueled a passion that was at once overwhelmingly urgent and bittersweet. She wept even as she reeled against the exhilarating play of his hands, gasping at the tide of fire that coursed through her. The sun filled her eyes, and the seawater seemed to burn and freeze her at once.

Matt, tall and strong against her, enveloped her, the corded muscles of his shoulders too wide for her fingers to encompass. She tested their texture, as smooth as warm marble, and then sought out his chest, the curling hair rasping against her. She wanted to taste all of him with her hands, as if she could drink in his scent and taste with her fingertips. The hard, flat torso, so soft in the seawater, so warm against starving hands. The strength of his thighs, the velvet-smooth steel that strained against her belly. She wanted all of him, like a glutton at a feast where the delights tasted were too delicious to imagine. The music of his moans only served to heighten her appetite. The play of his beautiful fingers against her aching breasts only urged her on.

He lifted her to him and she brought her arms around his neck needing to be as close to him as possible. She stroked his rich, dark hair and savored the smoldering light in his eyes as he cupped her bottom in one hand and let the other stray up along the soft underside of her thighs. His eyes in the full light of the sun were fierce, possessive. His fingers, so patient in the moonlight, commanded. They guided her surely, swirling and floating against satin recesses to unleash a sweet effervescence that was agony.

Even as Kelly strained against the hot convulsions he was unleashing in her, her mouth seeking his with her own fierce demand, Matt stoked the fires even higher. His hands trembling, he lifted her a little more and brought her legs around him, his mouth never leaving hers.

"Yes...yes," she whispered urgently, desperate to feel him inside her.

Matt gasped as he thrust into her, his arms crushing her against him. He uttered her name as his lips came down to meet hers. At that moment Kelly lost the sun. She lost the touch of the sea and the pull of memories. As she and Matt moved together, the quickening rhythm seeming to drive them impossibly closer, the brilliant agony forced her head back and her eyes open. She lost everything but the building explosion in her.

Matt buried his face in her throat with a sob and her hand came up to his head to hold him. She ached to be free of the savage fire that swept her, yet strained to be one with him. The inferno he'd unleashed consumed every nerve, even sweeping to her fingertips. It could not be contained. Then, when she thought she would have to beg Matt to free her, he brought his head up. Capturing her eyes with the fierce passion in his, he handed her the sun.

It ignited in her belly, deep where he filled her with a joy never imagined, a white-hot light that erupted and engulfed the world. The echo of her cries brought the cove back to life.

Then in silence he held her in his arms, her head resting on his shoulder. Tears stung again at Kelly's eyes. She didn't want to move, didn't ever want this moment to end. And yet she knew how futile that hope was even as the sound of a car far up on the road invaded the intimacy of their solitude. It was as if with that sound the outside world rushed back in.

Matt lifted his head and look down at her. For some reason his eyes were shadowed as if clouds had gathered to obscure their light. "Come on. We have to talk."

Kelly followed him to the beach, the idea of lying naked on a secluded beach alone with Matt seeming highly attractive.

The reality met and exceeded her expectations. The feeling of freedom was second in pleasure only to the sight of Matt's hard, lean body next to hers. She felt wonderfully hedonistic and slightly sinful. Before she'd met Matt she'd never allowed herself such liberty. It seemed that all of her responsibilities and commitments belonged to another world. Matt faced her and in his eyes Kelly saw the very things she wanted to escape on that fine, idyllic beach.

"Do you love Rich?" His eyes brooked no mischief. It seemed that the time was past for patience.

"What?"

"Do you love him as much as you love me?" he asked.

She heard a sharp intake of breath and realized it was her own. She tried mugging. "Are you sure *you* haven't been reading the papers?"

"Answer my question, Kelly."

Tears crowded her vision. She felt cornered, trapped. And she felt very small.

"I'm not sure it makes any difference, Matt."

"That's not what I asked, Kelly." His eyes held fire. "Tell me."

Kelly was snared, the throb of her pulse like a drum beat. She straightened, as if that would better help her to bear the pain of her words. "I didn't even love Michael as much as I love you."

For a long time, Matt was very still. He sat against a bare rock and sifted sand between his fingers. It almost looked as if he hadn't heard what Kelly said. When he spoke, his voice was so soft that Kelly almost couldn't hear it.

"Then I think you should know that I did a lot of thinking while I was away from you." He grinned briefly, his eyes wry. "Took a lot of cold showers, too, which is quite a feat where I was."

Kelly faced him, the scent of him still on her skin, the memory of his touch still sweet. She was going to tell him to stop before it was too late. Before there was no turning back. She saw the yearning in his eyes and lost her words.

"I've made a decision," he went on steadily, never looking away. "My mother's been telling me for years that I should grow up and find a good wife. I would have been happy to, if I'd only found someone I was madly in love with. A woman who made me believe in the Matt Hennessy I've always been, not just the one I've become." He reached over to her, his hand gently exploring the lines of her face. "I needed someone I missed so much in Greenland that I'd make the most involved plans since D-day just to trick her into meeting me in Hawaii for Christmas."

Kelly had begun to tremble, her eyes wide and stark. She heard his words and savored the feel of his hand. Then, with a tremulous grin, she reverted to her oldest defense. "Who?" she asked. "Missy?"

He grinned back, his eyes so full with love that Kelly thought they would engulf her. "Yes," he retorted evenly, "Miss. I came all this way to beg her to be our maid of honor. I'll break the news to her as soon as you say you'll marry me."

CHAPTER 13

K elly stood up and walked away toward the water. Suddenly self-conscious, she began donning the swimsuit, her fingers shaking too badly to properly tie the little strings.

"Kelly?"

Matt's voice behind her sounded soft and pleased. He stood up. She didn't speak, preoccupied with the task at hand and the sight of the sun skittering off the clear water—the sound of a pulsing tide that wasn't the ocean.

Matt moved closer. "Aren't you supposed to say something like 'Oh Matt dear, I'd love to marry you?'"

Kelly lifted her head and found that it didn't help her breathing. The sun hurt her eyes, and they suddenly filled with tears. When Matt moved to place his hands on her shoulders, she flinched and drew away.

"Talk to me, Kelly."

She finally turned to him, his face clouded and indistinct beyond the tears. "I'd like to go back, Matt," she managed, her voice balancing carefully with control. "I don't think I want to see Hana."

When she tried to take another breath, she made a

small, gasping sound as if the effort had proven painful. Matt took hold of her, his grasp too firm to shake loose, his eyes darker than she thought she'd ever seen them. A slate-gray ocean beneath a driving rain.

"Why do I have the feeling?" he said, his face close above hers, "that you're about to tell me no?"

She couldn't bear the pain in his eyes, but couldn't manage to look away. "I want to go home, Matt. I'm sorry, I just—"

"You love me," he challenged. "You just told me. And I love you more than my life. In some schools of thought that would be a perfectly good reason for proposing."

"I don't belong in your world," she tried, his touch robbing her breath. "I'm a nurse, not—"

"Kelly, don't give me that crap. Be honest. You're afraid. You've never felt this way about anyone and you don't know how to handle it."

She faced him mutely, but he knew her answer.

"And you think that because of what you've had to face in the past—" His eyes brooked no escape now "—because of what you hold yourself accountable for, you couldn't possibly deserve this much happiness."

Her small laugh sounded more like a sob. "Not exactly."

"Well, how do you think I feel?" he demanded. "I'm the man with everything he's ever wanted. Where does it say I get more than my allotment of happiness? But then, I guess it balances out. I had my choice of the most famous women in the world to date, offers from half the female population in the US to keep my bed warm, and I had the questionable sense to fall in love with the one woman who shows me up for the sham I am. I want to marry her so badly because I've been suffocating in that rarefied atmosphere, and I didn't even know it."

"I told you, you needed a better class of friends."

"You know what I mean."

She shook her head. "What do you suggest I do with all that excess emotional baggage I'm carrying around? My hands aren't sweating because of the humidity. I'm terrified. You say you love me, and I automatically brace myself for the next loss, the next load of guilt. Matt, you just can't imagine what kind of burden I carry around."

Instinctively he brought her into his arms, his head low over hers as if to protect her from the pain of her words. "It's only so much of a burden if you carry it alone," he said in a voice that pierced Kelly's heart.

She wanted to answer, to give voice to the panic, the joy, the love for him that swirled so hotly in her. But it seemed that the strength of his arms could really shut out the pain and ease the turbulence, like a great wall that stopped a fierce wind.

The hammering of her heart eased in her, and the oxygen she'd been struggling for finally found her lungs. She felt the broad strength of Matt's body against hers and soaked in its comfort. If only it were this easy. If only Matt was right, and he was strong enough to help her beat back the ghosts that plagued her.

She'd thought she couldn't love him more than she had before. She'd been wrong. His words filled her like a hot, white light. A sweet pain seemed to set the world around her alight in a beautiful new way.

"I'll tell you what," he said finally, looking down at her upturned face, his hand cupping her chin. "No answers now. But no escape, either. Come with me to Hana and we'll spend three days there as lovers. We'll sit and talk and make love and talk some more. Whatever you want to talk about. Then when we get back to the house, I'll ask you again. If you still want to go home then, you can." He grinned, gently brushing back an errant strand of hair from her forehead. "But I don't think you will."

Kelly tried to take a deep breath to steady herself. It didn't work. The emotions and conflicts bubbled up like a cauldron in her chest. She gave the answer she wanted to, before she let her common sense and fears get in the way. "It's a deal."

They finished the drive along the primitive, narrow road and checked into a hotel when they reached Hana. They swam, saw the sights, took a long walk on the quiet beach and ate dinner overlooking the sun as it slid into the ocean. All the while they talked of themselves, their jobs, their goals, the interests they had in common. They laughed and held hands and kissed.

After lingering over dinner and sitting out to watch the brilliant Hawaiian night from the lanai, after their questions had been answered and their doubts eased, Matt took Kelly into his arms, his eyes as soft as dawn, and he gentled her remaining fears with his hands. The wind washed them, and the night music drifted in the open balcony door. The half-moon lit Matt's face in the softest of lights and awoke the sleeping fires in Kelly.

They made love as if they'd just discovered each other, learning, without the distraction of the outside world, each other's needs and pleasures. Kelly, her head pillowed in Matt's arms, held him close, excited by the feel of him, comforted by the sanctuary of his embrace and moved by the words that he gave her.

They slept, still caught in each other's arms, and then woke to make love again.

Late in the night when the sounds of the sea served to lull them, they fell asleep. Kelly's cheek was pressed against the hollow of Matt's shoulder, legs curled against the pleasant roughness of his, her breathing synchronous with the sea. She knew that the night gave her courage, because she wanted suddenly to wake Matt to accept his proposal. She wanted to move into his world and share hers with him, and she wanted to tell him just how much of her life he'd become.

But she didn't. Lying very still against him, she waited for her own heart to calm and sleep to come. Maybe tomorrow she could tell him.

SHE KNEW INSTANTLY that this was the nightmare, the one that had chased and awakened her, sweating and afraid. She recognized the scene. Knew the outcome. And still she could not escape it.

Somewhere outside it was winter. Beyond the muted, sterile pastel of hospital walls, snow and sleet coated the roads like lethal icing, and the wind intensified the wet cold. Inside fake greenery and Christmas ornaments decorated the hallway. Bits of pretend cheer for the season.

Kelly had always liked to work nights. She stood now like a separate character waiting patiently for the ambulance to arrive. The room behind her was already set up. IV bags trailed lines like kite strings, and the crash cart waited at the head of the bed, drawers open and ready for the trauma patient they were expecting. Single car. Single victim. A man in his twenties. On tables at the sides of the room, sterilized battleship-blue instrument trays were piled like so many presents waiting to be opened.

The team had arrived from respiratory therapy and the lab. The chaplain, black-on-black, too shy and quiet yet to be comfortable with hospital humor, hovered in the background. The victim had run his compact car right off the highway and up against a tree. Head and chest injuries. The paramedics had reported his heart as still beating, even though his breathing was faltering and his pupils were fixed and dilated. Not much to do, but they'd do it. Young victims deserved that all ritual be carried out.

In her dream the light in the hallway seemed sharper, faces more clearly delineated. Missy was telling a particularly bad joke to the short, portly surgical resident who was renowned for his sick humor and vibrant blushes. The colors looked primary, primal, threatening. Kelly laughed with Missy as she picked up the mic to answer the latest call from the paramedics. But from somewhere beyond her, tension mounted. Fear crept in like a cold mist.

"This is 431." The voice floated free of static. "Patient has arrested. We have initiated CPR. ETA three minutes."

Now the movements slow, stretching gracefully like a dance. The hallway passes tile by tile beneath white-shod feet, voices garbled, laughing—tense with adrenaline and anticipation. The chaplain, so black against the vivid pastel, still hovers, unsure.

The door appears, sliding with a low, sighing whoosh to the sight of snow, white on flying white. Is it the wind or the ambulance siren that keens so? Kelly's hands chill and she rubs them together. The ambulance pulls to a sudden stop before her.

Kelly steps forward. The dream shrinks away, terror a living thing. The ensemble, a ballet troupe, tumbles about the stretcher and floats in slow motion to the room, over to where the swaying IV lines wait.

The resident's voice rises like smoke. "Let's take a look."

The troupe steps back, waiting.

And the certainty becomes reality.

"No!" Her own voice. Like the siren. "NOOO!"

Missy turns, her eyes a wasteland—trying to get hold, trying to help. His face, his dear, gentle face. His eyes open. Staring. The keening rises again, wild and savage, cutting even through the dream's terror.

And then, in the madness, when the room whirls into sound and loss the final terror. It is not Michael, dear, kind Michael, who lays shattered on the hard, lonely table.

It is Matt.

The keening follows her back, a high, terrible sound she remembered well.

When the hands caught her again, she fought like before, her rage a vicious thing. They couldn't hold her, she knew, but the realization was too much to bear.

"Kelly! Kelly, it's all right, wake up."

She fought, her mouth open, her grief a desolate sound. The hands held her close. Close and safe.

"Kelly, hush, it's a dream, hush."

He held her and rocked her like a baby, stroking her hair and cheek, easing her to consciousness.

Sanity crept back like a penitent child. The colors of the nightmare fled, and when Kelly opened her eyes the only sounds left were the rhythm of the ocean and Matt's soothing murmurs. Kelly gulped in air to still the battering of her heart against her chest wall. Her face was wet and her throat raw.

"Shhh," Matt whispered. "It's over now."

Abruptly Kelly sat up, away from him. His eyes mirrored anxiety. She could look at them only briefly before the terror hit her again, crushing her chest. Quickly, before Matt could object, she got up and dressed, her hands shaking, her vision blurred and melting.

"Kelly?" Matt slid over and swung his feet over the side of the bed.

She shied away, farther into the corner, the intensity of the dream still raging through her. Tears splashed on her hands and arms as she struggled into her clothes, and her breathing came in ragged, tearing gasps.

"Kelly, stop," he soothed, standing; approaching.

She whirled away from him. "Don't, Matt, I have to leave...I–"

"Kelly, calm down."

He approached again, towering above her in the darkened room.

"Please," she shrilled, cowering away, her hand up as if in protection. "I can't. I just...can't. As soon as I can, I'm going home."

When she'd pulled her clothes on she turned back to him, the desolation in her eyes encompassing him. "I should never have tried. I can't do it, Matt. I'm just not that strong."

And catching hold of the door handle, she opened it and fled.

CHAPTER 14

Matt caught up with her far down the beach. She didn't know where she thought she would go to escape him in the predawn gray; she just knew that she had to get away. The nightmare pursued her, its vivid scenes flashing before her tear-blurred eyes with relentless repetition. Even after Michael's death the dream had never been so vivid, so devastating.

It had been over a year since she'd awakened screaming into the desolation of the night as if screaming would purge the raging grief. She'd thought the nightmares had been easing, fading away as she'd gathered courage to go on.

She'd been wrong.

They had been the warnings—the signal that her awakening attachment to Matt would prove disastrous. She should have known, should have listened to the small voice that had tried to protect her from the pain.

To the east, the sky began to lighten, the ocean paling beneath it. Kelly walked on, still fleeing, her breathing still ragged with the tears of loss. She never heard him approach. His hands were just suddenly on her shoulders.

"Are you going to walk back home?"

Kelly closed her eyes against the comfort of his touch, and pulled away. "I needed to walk. I'll hire a car when I can, and drive back."

"In Hana? Highly doubtful. I do know a guy with a helicopter service. A little expensive, but he'll get you there."

"Fine."

"Do I at least get an explanation?"

Kelly wanted to turn to him then, to seek the solace she knew she would find in his eyes, but she didn't have the strength. The sight of those eyes, lifeless, still tormented her.

"The nightmares I've been having," she began, her voice quiet, her eyes looking out to the sea and the soft light of dawn. "The ones I couldn't remember. Came in sharp and clear this time."

She couldn't go on for a moment.

"Michael's death?"

She turned on him, torment flashing through the tears. "Yes. A playback of that night in lurid, living detail. Working on him and then suddenly recognizing him. An ER nurse's most horrible fear. I almost lost my mind."

"You had the guts to stay there and go on with your job."

She shrugged. "I'm an emergency room nurse. We're funny like that. Spoiled for anything else. It has nothing to do with guts."

His eyes, so infinitely gentle, sought out the despair in hers. "I disagree. I don't think you give yourself enough credit. Or me enough of a chance." Almost unconsciously, he reached out to touch the tears on her cheek, as if by accepting their weight he was assuming her grief. "Together we can get beyond the trauma of the past."

Kelly shook her head, the tears clogging her throat and clouding her vision. "No, Matt," she whispered, "you don't understand. It wasn't the past in that nightmare, and that's what made it so awful. See, Michael wasn't the one in my dream this time. You were." Her voice broke completely then, and she was only able to whisper the rest, the most important. "I'm sorry. I'm just not strong enough for that. I have to leave."

For a moment there was silence between them. The sun rose behind Kelly and shot tiny flames into Matt's eyes. He didn't touch her, didn't move to hold her. She stood rigidly before him, aching for the feel of his arms and yet knowing that if he moved to touch her, she'd run.

Finally he spoke without taking his eyes from her. "I'll help you get back." His voice and face were quiet. "I'll book you a room in a hotel if you can't stay at the house and I'll get you on the first possible flight back to St. Louis. But I think I should warn you. I'm not going to let you get on that plane without me."

She stared at him, stunned. "You promised."

He shrugged, a hesitant grin touching his face. "I lied. I'm not going to let you do this to yourself. I love you too much. You're going to have to end up marrying me."

Matt did just as he promised. He hired a helicopter, rode with her back to Lahaina and booked a room for her. The flight he got her would leave the next day. He was just as diligent in keeping the rest of his promise.

During the short flight he tried to reason with her. At the hotel room he tried extravagant promises. He even tried guilt, arguing that his mother would never forgive her for deserting the family before Christmas. When he left to pick up her things from the house, he warned her that he would pick up right where he left off when he got back.

When Matt returned, Kelly was sitting silently out on the lanai watching the endless play of the surf against the beach. She hardly noticed when he walked in and didn't answer when he passed on messages of outrage from everyone at her decision. Finally he walked up to stand just behind her, not touching her. Kelly lifted her head fractionally, but she kept her silence.

"I'm going to leave you alone now," he said without preamble. "But I want you to think about something. If you marry someone like Rich, you won't be taking any risks. Because you won't love him. But ask yourself one question before you make that decision. Is the price for that lifelong security worth it? I think you're going to be more dead married to someone else than you would if you took a chance on me and lost me like you did Michael."

Matt didn't see the tears that again coursed down Kelly's cheeks. She offered the sea a small shrug. "I guess I'm just not the gambling type anymore."

There was a long silence behind her.

"I'll be here tomorrow to take you to the airport."

Now there was no mistaking the tears. "I'd rather you didn't."

He didn't say good-bye when he left.

An hour later, the phone rang. Kelly walked into the room to get it, knowing perfectly well who it was.

"Just what the hell do you think you're doing? Do you have any idea what you've just done? I credited you for having at least some sense. I haven't seen anything that dumb since Humphrey Bogart opted for the French underground over Ingrid Bergman. My God, Kelly, this is the man who's going to save your life!"

When Kelly spoke, it seemed to take a great effort. "Missy, shut up. I've made up my mind. You stay here and finish your vacation."

"You're damn right I'm staying...! Kid, you sound awful. How about if I come over and we'll go to an old movie together or something."

"No." Kelly took a breath. The great weight she felt made even breathing a struggle. "I'd rather be alone, Miss. Thanks. I'll see you at home."

"Okay, but I still—"

"Bye, Miss."

Kelly hung up and was about to call the operator to hold any more calls. She stood there, the phone beneath her hand, the import of the words she'd just said seeping into her like vile, decaying water. She'd just given away her last chance at life and she knew it. She was just too afraid to take that chance, too afraid to face the possibility of that nightmare becoming reality.

For the first time, she saw clearly what she faced. She would go back and spend her life in gray monotony with someone else, ending up by making his life as miserable as hers. And when they had children, she would pass along to them that same apathy, that same fear of challenging life she'd succumbed to. In the end she would hate herself as much as them for the choices she'd made in this hotel room.

For a moment longer she looked down at the phone, her breathing faster, more labored. The sobs that had plagued her rose in her chest and burned with a hot, terrible fire. Her hands trembled with pain. The consequence of her decision built in her like steam in a faulty boiler until she knew that something would blow.

Suddenly without knowing how or why, she had the phone in both hands. She ripped at it, hauled, yanked until the whole unit snapped out of the wall socket. Then with a pitcher's move she hurled it away from her, as if it were at fault for the agony that consumed her. The phone hit the wall with a dull ringing noise and fell to the soft carpet with a muffled thud. Kelly looked around her, the need for physical release even more acute. She found a few books, a makeup case, a glass, the plastic water pitcher that was standard in any hotel room. All followed the phone. She threw harder and harder until she was panting with the exertion. Great heaving sobs tore at her as she threw, the emotion bubbling up with the release of the actions.

The glass was last. With a splintering crash it shattered against the wallpaper like a bomb. The noise brought Kelly up sharp. Someone would be in here shortly to take her away if she didn't stop. A small pile of destroyed articles lay scattered around the floor as if cast there by a great wind. Kelly stared at them dumbly, surprised at the destruction, sobs still catching her breath in uneven gasps.

She stayed as she was for a long time, letting her racing heart slow, her breathing ease, the rage die in her chest. Then she walked back out to the lanai and sat down.

The sun had reached its zenith and begun its slide into the ocean. Clouds stretched along the horizon like long banners, lit with the dying fires of the setting sun. The ocean glowed and glittered, reflecting the coral, the crimson and finally magenta sky as the sun disappeared over the horizon. It seemed as if there had never been a more beautiful sunset, as if its fingers reached out to draw its beholders into the softening hues of dusk and hold them there, bewitched.

Through it all Kelly sat quietly, not reacting. Images of the day before reeled through her mind. Matt's touch, the way his eyes crinkled at the corners like a little boy's when he smiled, the almost gluttonous way he attacked life. He had awakened in her a passion for life she'd never known existed. It was as if she'd survived only in a functional way before without really savoring the flavor of life. She'd lived in a black-and-white world until Matt had come along with his color camera. Now that he'd walked out the door, the life again died in her.

But then just as vividly she saw his face as he'd lain on the hard table in her dream, and the pain of it knifed savagely through her again. She hadn't exaggerated. She really wasn't sure she could survive losing Matt. She still had to think that it would be better to get away from him before she couldn't leave at all. She would go away and just survive in black-and-white.

Throughout the night Kelly remained where she was, not noticing the lush rhythm of the sea, or the insect song, or the moon as it arced in crystal flight over the black sea. She didn't feel the discomfort of sitting in one place too long, nor did she have the energy left to get up and move to her bed. She simply sat, her dry eyes burning, a yawning emptiness growing and echoing in her.

Toward dawn, when only the ocean spoke and the moon had left the sky black and shivering with starlight, Kelly dozed. The pain and confusion of her decision followed relentlessly.

At six o'clock a porter knocked on the door to notify her that her phone was out of order. He saw the

debris strewn across the room and the dying light in
Kelly's eyes and made no comment. Then he handed
over the airline ticket that had been left for her, rattling off arrangements. Kelly watched as if he were
speaking a foreign language then stood aside as he
picked up her bags and preceded her out the door.

She followed to the cab and sat in silence all the
way to the airport. There she nodded and followed
along as airline officials shuffled her toward the plane.
She followed instructions and mumbled her thanks,
but her eyes were watching for a promise to be kept.

No one appeared. No white horse or brass band,
no madman charging the gate at the last minute to
keep her from boarding. Kelly walked up the steps
with a growing distress she recognized as grief. And
when the doors closed and the plane began to taxi for
takeoff, she finally admitted to herself that she'd
hoped against hope that Matt would come for her,
saving her from the devastation of her future the way
Lancelot had whisked Guinevere away from her death
at the last minute. Matt wouldn't come though, and
Kelly would be left to bear the consequences of her
decision.

~

IT HAD SNOWED IN ST. Louis while she'd been gone.
Everywhere she turned, newscasters were gleefully
anticipating a white Christmas. Kelly couldn't stand it.
All of the false cheer made her want to scream. As
much as she feared the emptiness of her home, it was
the only haven she had. She pulled into her driveway
and climbed out, too numb and tired to even think.

The rooms were cold, the furniture harder than
she remembered. She forgot to turn on any lights

when she went in to sit on the couch and wait for the sun to struggle into a winter sky. Oh God, she thought with closed eyes and open mouth. Did it hurt this much when I lost Michael? Did I really feel so empty?

Kelly found herself back on her feet. She couldn't stay here, either. The thick silence was smothering her. The air carried such memories of Matt that she actually anticipated his scent. Maybe she'd go into work and see what was going on. Ask if they needed any help. Yeah, right. They wouldn't be curious about why Kelly showed up a week early. She'd just tell them the truth. That she'd discovered she had an allergy to coconuts and had spent her time in the islands sneezing.

First, though, she'd brew a pot of coffee and let the caffeine get her sleep-starved body back into gear. Again.

She was standing in the kitchen rubbing at burning eyes and fighting the urge to get back on the next plane. The smell of coffee filled the room, a rich, pungent aroma that should have conjured up pleasant morning memories. It made Kelly think of Matt. The tears threatened again, hot and painful. Why had she thought the pain would ease as she piled up the miles away from Matt? It had only grown worse.

She had just removed the coffeepot when the doorbell rang. She raised her head, startled. Kelly looked toward the living room as the bell sounded again. Short, insistent jabs. Maybe if she ignored it, whoever it was would leave, figuring she was asleep. She turned back to her coffee and poured a cup. The person didn't seem to understand that she didn't want company. They'd given up on decorum and star ted pounding on the door.

When the message became ringing, pounding and door rattling, Kelly gave in.

"All right," she muttered, coffee in hand as she began to unlatch. "All right. You win."

Then she pulled the heavy door open and froze. Before she could give voice to any of the half dozen emotions ignited, she found herself in Matt's arms.

"God, Kelly, you scared me," he was saying, his face buried in her hair, his grip on her frantic. "Why the hell didn't you answer the door?"

She couldn't quite account for the silly smile on her face. "Probably because I wasn't up for any emotional scenes. You know how crabby I am when I miss my sleep."

She placed the coffee cup down, and her arms went up to circle his back. That strong, solid back that could help carry such burdens.

"You came all this way for me?"

Matt lifted his head, his eyes still liquid for his moment of fear. "I trekked from Greenland to Hawaii for you. This is small bananas."

"But you let me get on the plane. You promised you wouldn't."

He brought his hand up to her cheek. "You wanted me to stop you?"

She grinned ruefully, the tears of relief now splashing onto her arms. "I guess I did. I'm sorry, Matt. I'm sorry I put you through this."

He brushed her hair back and kissed her forehead, the touch of his lips like the taste of water on the desert.

"You didn't put me through anything," he insisted. "I'm the one who should be sorry. I pushed too hard after all. I was going to do it again at the airport. Had a band and everything to serenade you in front of half of Honolulu. Mom talked me out of it. She was the one who suggested I just get on the plane and follow you here so we could be alone."

"You were on the plane?" she demanded. "Why didn't I know?"

He grinned. "I traveled tourist. Incognito. Quite a leveling experience."

"That's all right," she retorted with a grin. "You needed it."

The humor left his eyes. "Not as much as I needed you. I watched you, Kelly. Last night and then on the plane. I don't ever want you to have to look like that again."

Kelly settled more comfortably into his arms and ran a hand over the solid planes of his face. The bubble was back, that bright balloon that could crowd her chest with its shiny silver. She took a deep breath, savoring the scents in her home and thinking that as long as she lived she would delight in waking up early in the morning for coffee and the sweet sea of Matt's eyes. As long as she had him next to her, laughing and strong, she could face the uncertainties of the future and put away the pain of the past.

What surprised her was that even as battered as her body felt, it could still react so predictably to contact with Matt's. Letting the realization fill her eyes, she faced him, her fingers finding the buttons of his shirt.

"It might be something we could work on," she suggested, dropping her face to savor the skin she was uncovering.

Matt didn't seem at all averse to the direction the conversation was taking. Letting his own arms drop a little, he slid his hands up beneath her blouse to the sensitive skin at her waist. His lips found her ear and unleashed a shiver as he nibbled on the soft shell.

"I like the way you attack a problem," he said breathlessly, his fingers now at her buttons.

When his arms brushed against her breasts, it was to find the nipples already taut. Kelly's head came up as Matt slid the blouse from her arms. His lips moved to her throat, and she shivered, her knees going rubbery. Sparks seemed to leap from his fingertips as they pulled the straps of her bra over her arms.

Kelly dropped her head back. "Can you guarantee me you won't...oh...."

He was kissing her shoulder, then moving back to her neck, nibbling at the tender skin and then tracing designs with his tongue. Then he found her breasts and sent shock waves through her as he took her nipples between finger and thumb and massaged.

"That you won't leave me again," she finally managed between kisses.

"Oh," he answered, sounding just as breathless.

He paused to unbutton her skirt and slide it past her hips, his hands pausing to inflame the curves and hollows and send Kelly to gasping. "I imagine I'll die someday, but I won't go far till then."

She felt his hands on her hips again, sliding her panties down. She was becoming so impatient to have the feel of him against her that she almost told him to just rip them.

"But I'll promise you one thing."

Kelly stood against him, her belly against the strong warmth of his, amused that even through the material of his slacks he seemed to radiate heat like a furnace. He brought his hands back up, testing the smoothness of her leg, his fingers deliciously calloused as they first traveled up the inside of her thigh then traced patterns along her stomach. As his fingers discovered the hot core he'd ignited, she could only manage a mumbled answer. "Mmmmm?"

He moved to hold her then, bringing her chin up so she would face him. She opened her eyes and was again overwhelmed by the depth of emotion in those fathomless eyes.

"You and I will live more in one day than anyone else does in a lifetime. That way when one of us does die, the other won't have anything to regret."

For a long moment they stood still, the breadth of their love communicated in electric silence. It was as if the warm coffee-scented air sheltered them from the outside world.

"You know," Kelly finally said, her head tilted up to him, eyes bright and smiling, "I think you might just be right."

Matt smiled and bent to kiss her, his lips and tongue searching hers as if discovering a new taste. "No more arguments?"

She shook her head, her attention on the belt she was unfastening. "More of an observation, actually."

He slid his hands around to the soft mounds on her bottom. "What?"

She grinned. "I'm glad I'm already undressed. I don't think I could wait."

He laughed and swung her into his arms. "Me neither."

EPILOGUE

Kelly woke to the sunlight and the sounds of wind and sea. Wonderful sounds, she thought. Wonderful feeling. Air that washed over her like a fresh promise, and a sun so warm it nourished. What a way to wake up. Every morning perfect, every moment alive. Everyone should wake up feeling this way.

She stretched languorously and savored a few extra moments alone in bed. Outside the window she saw that clouds had begun to mass for a morning shower. Splendid soft things that climbed and tumbled over the sky and shrouded the mountains in a mist. In the early-morning light, their color and form seemed new and breathtaking. Kelly wondered how she'd never noticed before. She was so enthralled with her new perception of life that she didn't hear the sound of the door open.

"You look like a saint having a vision," Missy offered dryly. "I don't know if I'm going to be able to stand you like this."

"You're right." Kelly grinned brightly, sitting up. "It is pretty disgusting, isn't it?"

Missy surveyed her for a moment and shook her

head. "And to think that it's all my fault. I could have saved you from all this by just refusing to come here for vacation like your better sense suggested."

Then unable to hold off any longer, she grinned, too, her eyes full of a sparkling light. Missy couldn't bear to see her family unhappy. She plopped down alongside Kelly, her knees drawn up to her chest. "So, have you decided what you're going to do with your house yet? I'd offer to buy it, but I've decided that I kinda like the name Missy Hennessy, so I thought I'd give Tim a run for his money. After all, Barbara told me that I'm expected at all the family functions from now on anyway. I might as well try and make it official." Kelly could have sworn at that point that Missy's eyes misted up on her, something Missy abhorred since it threatened her meticulous makeup. "Ya know, I think this is going to be the Christmas we've been looking for all these years, kid. I told you there wasn't anything in Keystone but snow. We should have come here all along. Did you call your dad?"

Kelly wasn't in the least thrown by Missy's abrupt change in subject. She nodded thoughtfully. "Yesterday while you and Tim were playing sea monster and Annette Funicello."

"He was happy, wasn't he?"

Kelly nodded. "Yeah. He said maybe I'd like to use Mom's gown."

Maybe it was time to go to Chicago, too. There was an awful lot she wanted to say to her father.

"It'll be beautiful on you." Missy smiled. "You dad's going to give you away?"

Kelly just nodded, her father's painfully stiff words of love still caught in her chest.

Just then Emily popped her head in the door. "C'-

mon, you guys, we're gonna open presents. Aren't you coming?"

Kelly grinned. "Soon as I get dressed, Em."

The girl grimaced dramatically. "You'll look awfully dumb. We always open our presents in our pajamas. Like we're still kids, ya know?"

"Okay, thanks, squirt." She used Emily's brothers' pet name for her. Emily graced them with another grimace before disappearing.

Missy grinned after her. "I could sure get used to having her around. She wants to visit me in St. Louis over spring break. She says if I show her my emergency room, she'd introduce me to Uncle Paul. Newman. Uncle Paul, for God's sake. She introduces me to her Uncle Paul, I'll *give* her my emergency room. Ya know, she almost walked over to your hotel when she heard you were trying to pull the great escape. Then again, so did Barbara and John. Only my cool sense and Matt's threats kept them from storming the gates."

"You've told me." The thought of their concern still gave Kelly comfort.

"I just wish I could have been along. Just for the ride, you understand."

"Of course. For the day you ghostwrite my amazing life story."

Missy scowled. "Can't hardly do that when I don't know the inside story of the great reconciliation."

Kelly's smile was passive. "Inconvenient, I know."

"Or why you missed two scheduled flights back and had to end up chartering your own."

"Car trouble."

Another scowl. "You know the information's safe with me. I'd only sell it for top dollar. But that's okay, don't tell your best friend."

Kelly couldn't help her own smug grin. "Oh well, if that's the case then, okay. I won't."

"Well," Missy said, flying neatly off in yet another direction, "are you ready to open your presents with all the other kids?"

Kelly grinned greedily, happily anticipating her first Christmas morning since she was eighteen. "Oh, all right, if you insist."

By the time the two of them got there, everyone had gathered in the living room where a six-foot pine tree stood, having been erected and decorated the night before. The star that topped it still leaned precariously to one side after Matt had performed his "star-topping-Christmas-tree-with-star" routine after drinking half a bowl of eggnog. Kelly, who had enjoyed much of the remaining half, had fallen asleep in the middle of it all. In an attempt to get her attention Matt had tripped over the light cord and almost downed the whole tree. No one had had the presence of mind to correct the leaning star.

This morning the big windows were open to let the breeze wash through, the rain shower already passed. Palm trees dipped gently along the shore, and the Christmas temperatures would be in the eighties. The Hennessy family sat in bathrobes and slippers with small caches of presents before them, and soft strains of "White Christmas" drifted over from the stereo. Kelly couldn't think of anything more incongruous. Even so, she caught herself grinning again, and thought that she must look silly. She just kept wanting to giggle with the unaccustomed flush of anticipation that flooded her. She hadn't sat in a living room on Christmas morning like this for an eternity. And until a few days ago, it had seemed that she never would again. She did feel like a child who was opening her first Christmas present. As if all of her life lay ahead of her.

Matt sat down next to her on the floor and handed her a cup of coffee. His smile told her how he cherished her excitement. "Having a good time?"

She smiled over at him, basking in the light of his eyes. "I know it's a cliche, but I keep waiting to wake up."

"Don't you dare," he chastised. "I'm getting too used to spending all this money for it to be a dream."

Matt's words stopped Kelly, a sudden comprehension caught in her chest like a thief who'd had the lights turned on him.

"What's the matter?" Matt immediately asked.

His parents heard his concern and looked over.

Kelly grinned sheepishly at them all and then turned her attention back to Matt. "It's just that I hadn't really thought about it, I guess."

"Thought about what?"

"Well, uh, you're quite...uh, wealthy, aren't you?"

Matt grinned with delight at her discomfort. "Quite. Does that change things?"

"I don't know. I'm still trying my damnedest to get used to your occupation!"

Matt put his arm around her. "It's all right. If you'd like, we'll live off your salary and I'll donate mine to charity."

"No. That's okay." She smiled sweetly. "I was just trying to say that I wasn't used to the idea. Not that I found it unacceptable."

"Good—" Matt grinned "—I don't think your salary could support this house and the one in Carmel."

Kelly gaped. "Carmel?"

He nodded. "Tim's been taking care of it for me.

There's also the apartment in London and the ranch in Wyoming."

"And the house in St. Louis. I want to keep that, too."

Matt nodded. "An excellent idea."

"Don't forget Gstaad," Tim spoke up with a complacent grin.

Matt nodded. "Thanks, that too."

"Enough," Kelly protested, a hand raised. "Until three days ago, I was still worried about how to fix the plumbing in my house. Can we take this slowly?"

"Sure," he agreed, dropping a kiss on her head. "We just have to decide where we're going to live before we get married. Now open your Christmas present."

She accepted a package from him and studied it. About shoe box size, it was neatly wrapped in blue foil and felt fairly light. Kelly undid the ribbon and tried her best not to tear the paper. That little-boy look was in Matt's eyes again, and everyone else was suddenly very quiet. Kelly had the feeling something important was in the box.

Unconsciously holding her breath against finding something like the emeralds, she lifted the lid. No one spoke. Matt's grin broadened noticeably.

Nestled in a bed of tissue paper, a little egg-shaped doll smiled up at Kelly with unblinking, painted eyes. Her dress, also brightly painted, seemed to be a quaint native outfit with layers of intricately designed flowers covered by a white apron. Kelly looked up at Matt.

"She's a matryoshka," he explained, motioning for her to pick up the gift. "It's a little Russian doll. I saw her at one of the airports and couldn't resist. It opens. Try it."

Kelly did, pulling the doll neatly in half. Inside

was another identical doll, only smaller. Kelly couldn't help but smile.

"She's darling," she agreed as again the doll opened to reveal another and yet another smaller version, the detail lovingly miniaturized. At the end Kelly held the smallest doll, the size of her thumb, and its five sisters of graduating size in her lap.

"She's beautiful, Matt. Thank you."

She was moving to put the doll back together again when Matt caught her hand. "Wait a minute," he protested. "You haven't found out all about her yet. Keep going."

Kelly looked up at him, then at the doll. "There's another one?"

"Well, look."

She did, but when she pulled the little doll apart, a smaller doll didn't tumble into her lap as before. A ring did.

Kelly gasped, not moving. There, winking up at her from the dark fabric of her robe, was a round solitaire diamond set in a thin gold band. Kelly was no real judge but she thought it was a carat; flawless and blue, breathtaking. Simple perfection.

Without waiting for Kelly, who still hadn't remembered to breathe, Matt picked the ring up and slipped it onto her shaking finger.

"It was my grandmother's," he told her, his eyes bright with excitement. "Is it all right?"

Kelly faced him with a smile, even as tears spilled over onto the hand he held. "I thought that the Hennessy tradition demanded a box of Cracker Jacks."

"I thought of that." He nodded "But that had been done. Besides, you would have known before you opened it. If there's one thing I'm going to strive for in our relationship, it's originality."

"Does that mean that I can anticipate this kind of thing from now on?"

"Like I told you," he said with a smile that excluded everyone else, "every minute of every day we're alive."

"I love it." She smiled, seeing no one but him. "And I love you, too."

Matt pulled her close and kissed her to the sound of family applause.

"Now comes the mushy part," Kelly heard Missy say.

Emily groaned. "Oh, gross!"

Kelly laughed and thought how wonderful it felt to be alive again.

ALSO BY EILEEN DREYER

Korbel Classics Wounded Hero Collection

Jake's Way

Simple Gifts

Timeless

Perchance To Dream

A Soldier's Heart

A Rose For Maggie

Korbel Classics Humorous Collection

The Ice Cream Man

Isn't It Romantic?

A Prince of A Guy

The Princess & The Pea

A Fine Madness

Drakes Rakes

Barely A Lady

Never A Gentleman

Always A Temptress

It Begins With A Kiss

Once A Rake

Twice Tempted

Mystery and Suspense

A Man To Die For

Nothing Personal

Brain Dead
Bad Medicine
If Looks Could Kill

ABOUT THE AUTHOR

EILEEN DREYER/*KATHLEEN KORBEL* is a New York Times bestselling, award-winning author who blames her writing on an Irish heritage that gave her the desire and a supportive husband who gave her the ultimatum, "Do something productive or knock it off." It worked. She has published about 50 books and short stories in suspense and various romance sub-genres, her newest foray being into what she likes to call Historical Romantic Adventure.

Besides enjoying her family, she loves to travel and travels to research. It's her excuse and she'd sticking to it, certain that she'll find a story that provides an excuse for riding elephants in India, climbing Macchu Piccu and singing traditional Irish music on four continents. She also has animals, but refuses to submit them to the limelight.

www.ingramcontent.com/pod-product-compliance
Lightning Source LLC
Chambersburg PA
CBHW011514100726
47899CB00010BD/3365

* 9 781648 392795 *